CHASING TRUTH IN A HARBOR TOWN

WILLIAM BRENNAN

THM

Ten Hut Media
tenhutmedia.com

ISBN: 978-1-96400-789-2 (Paperback)

ALSO BY WILLIAM BRENNAN

Michael Lund Series

Chasing Truth in a Harbor Town

Never miss a new release!

To find out more about William Brennan and his books, visit

severnriverbooks.com/collections/william-brennan

For Frances

1

"I'm coming for you."

Michael Lund clicked the phone off in reply and placed it in the pocket of his deer-blood stained Carhartt. Down the hill, a lake freighter sailed at reduced speed out of Duluth's harbor with its iron ore cargo. A light snow drifted through still air. The cold was there, too. It escaped from the icy pavement into the bones of his feet. They creaked like the freighter's hull.

Michael would have broken contact with Nikolai and Kristelena by now if he was afraid. He often wondered, as he did now, what he would do if another path into the secret world presented itself. It always came back to the question of who Nikolai and Kristelena really were and which interests they served. Whichever powers they may have answered to, he was certain they didn't reside within the United States.

He failed to register the words coming from the tender, familiar voice behind him as he watched the freighter slog its way into the approaching night. "What's that, Sue?"

"I asked if Nikolai is picking you up for your hockey game tonight." Sue walked down the freshly shoveled concrete steps of the nineteenth-century brick apartment building. She wore her mother's stitched snow boots and her sandy blond hair down under a knit stocking hat.

"He's on his way. I was just on the phone with him." Michael flicked a bit of snow at Sue with the blade of his hockey stick. She dodged it, bending athletically at her hip.

"Nice aim, at least you're handsome if you can't score any goals." She smiled at him, parting her ample lips. "Are you still getting your Russian practice in with Nikolai?"

"I try to keep up. It's hard to get back into it." Michael rested his freshly shaven, hockey scarred chin on the knob of his hockey stick. "Handsome, huh?" He knew she was the beautiful one of the pair. The winter's cold brought out a rosiness in her cheeks.

"You probably haven't spoken more than ten words of it since college, maybe just the odd 'durak' when you're watching a game and the other team scores." Sue grabbed the hockey stick and started twirling it in her gloved hands. "What does that mean again?"

"It means 'fool'," Michael said. "Nikolai and Kristelena speak Russian faster than anyone did in class."

"Did you catch what they were saying at the tennis court before we officially met them? They were loud."

"Mostly just repeating some lines from a Deti Rave song from what I could tell."

An engine groan cut through the air. "I can hear that car coughing from a mile away," Michael said. He looked down the hill, following a string of spotty streetlights. Nikolai's '84 Volvo station wagon gained ground, paying for every inch.

"How does he drive that in Duluth?" Sue asked. "This town is one big hill."

"He says the conditions are too bad here to drive anything worth over a thousand dollars."

Nikolai put the car in park and hit the horn. The muffler rattled as the car idled, dribbling brown sweat on the packed snow below.

"Tell him it's Sunday night, Michael, and families are trying to get the kids down."

As if he heard, Nikolai looked over at Sue from inside the car and gave a sheepish smile. It could have been because of a look she gave back that he put a finger over his mouth and made a shooshing impression.

Sue raised her eyebrows as Michael approached to kiss her goodbye. Their lips were cold. The kiss was sweet, bringing lips to life.

Michael set his equipment in the back of the car and dropped down into the passenger seat. "Does this thing even get over sixty?"

"You can joke, but not about my car." Nikolai shook his head and finger simultaneously. They pulled away from the snowbank with a sputter and drove toward Highway 35. At one of the factories they passed on their route, night-shift workers parked their cars and shuffled slowly to the entrance through a turbulent and unforgiving January wind. Winter had arrived late this year but was quick to turn bitter.

"Tell me again how you and Kristelena ended up here in this liver-colored town," Michael said. He tried to turn up the heat in the car, but the dial was already at its limit. It wobbled and fell into his hand. He pressed it back into place before Nikolai could see and put one hand on each of the passenger-side air vents.

"You know why." Nikolai jerked the wheel, avoiding a pothole forged by successive Minnesota winters. He pushed the gas pedal and a disproportionate amount of grey smoke escaped from the exhaust pipe, filling the rearview mirror. The car grumbled.

"Because that Gregory guy offered you jobs and a place to stay? You couldn't find anyone else to help you out? Don't get me wrong, we're glad to have you on our hockey team."

"We're dentists. Gregory gave us the chance to stay in our world as dental assistants. He also gave us a room and a car," Nikolai said as he patted the steering wheel and gave his habitual friendly grin.

"We don't mind the cold. We're used to freezing winters and short days. Moscow isn't exactly Cancun."

"Neither is Duluth, Niky. By the way, most Russians I've met don't smile like you. Where'd you pick that up? Cancun?"

"Funny. I adjusted to the culture here. Kristelena and I practiced in the mirror. Now we have smile contests. It's kind of like a staring contest but you feel more like...lunatic. As dentists, we love the smiles, it shows off hard work."

"Were you able to sell your things before you left Moscow?"

"Kristelena's Saab, our flat, most of our clothes. We didn't get the best deal. We're just glad we made it here before Covid and Putin's invasion, even if northern Minnesota is the Siberia of America."

"At least there are plenty of trees in Siberia to block the wind. When are you going to invite me to look at Gregory's shed? Doesn't he collect vintage cars or something?"

"He runs a small import business on the side. Things like cars, pottery, carpets. He sells a lot of pottery on Etsy. Kristelena and I have to help him package, and we give him shit that we are like indentured servants for his Etsy business. He doesn't think that's funny. He keeps asking us for help, though, so we keep telling him, 'Gregory, we are going to put a note in one of these pots saying that you've forced us to package these goods and all you give us in return is some mushroom soup that tastes like the floor, like dirt.' You will come sometime, and we can sauna, too. We will show you how we live."

Inside Heritage Arena, the dressing room was full. The hooks were crowded with parkas, denim jeans, and hockey pants waiting to be thrown on before hitting the hard ice.

"Hey, take those boots off at the door, fellas," Paul, the jaunty team captain, said as Nikolai and Michael stepped into the room. "I lost an edge last game because one of you clowns dragged in a rock from your shoes. Niky sweet hands, Niky pick pocket, got any goals left in that stick? We'll work on the nickname."

"Maybe it's just Nick...but yes, there should be goals left in this old thing. Maybe an assist for you as well. There should have been one last week." Nikolai studied his stick, avoiding Paul's challenging glare.

"Didn't you see the hook on me?" Paul asked, wide-eyed. "Anyway, just count yourself lucky that Chris is having knee surgery and we let you use his gear this season. This guy..." Paul finished taping his blade and broke the canvas tape off with his teeth, tossing the roll into his open bag, which was littered with yellow-tinted pads.

Some people are hockey players, and some people play hockey. The difference is in the details. Nikolai, as they all knew, was a hockey player. Russians are deceptive. They have the finesse of Swedes but the temper of Canadians. Nikolai had yet to show any kind of physical aggression. He was in total control, but buried safely somewhere within his solid six-foot, 200-pound frame and beneath his dentist's smile, there was an undeniable ability to inflict a sort of harm that had no place in a hockey rink, and he kept it locked away.

"A lot of hockey in Moscow, I'm sure. Right, Nick?" Paul said. Briefly naked, he pulled his off-white jock strap on with a snap and stood at attention.

"There is not so much hockey in Moscow. Too many people, not enough ice. I'm from Yaroslavl originally, where hockey is important. It has had a team in the highest league in Russia going back to the Soviet Championship League in the 1960s. I never played for them, but my grandfather played for the team back then, and my uncle played for Lokomotiv later. The game is in my blood as you say."

The warmups were lazy. Paul strutted along the red line, crossing over it occasionally to incite the other team. "Bring your aspirin for when I catch you coming across the middle tonight?" he asked in the vague direction of the opposing players.

At the face-off dot, Nikolai lined up at right wing with a forward lean. He wore his socks in the Euro style with skate tongue and Achilles guard tucked inside.

The goateed referee released the puck, the draw was won back to Michael, and Nikolai circled behind the opposing defense. Finding a seam between the defense, Michael sent Nikolai to the net with a low and fast pass. Speeding in with his long strides, Nikolai slipped the puck behind the goaltender on his backhand.

"*Otlichna!*" Michael yelled as he skated to Nikolai.

"*Spacibo.*" Nikolai said, fully enunciating for Michael's benefit before returning to the face-off dot.

In the lively dressing room after the game, Paul lifted a can of pilsner to 'our Russian spy.' The room cheered loud enough for the opposing team to hear and beat the thin, paint-chipped, wooden wall that separated them. Michael raised his can with steady eyes and a sliver of a smile.

2

The same Sunday evening, Sue trudged through a winter fog towards Varmland's Wine Bar, where she was meeting Kristelena. The air was bitter and dense. She hunched her shoulders, guarding her neck from the cold, until they stiffened and seemed to become stuck permanently at her ears.

She crossed the street after the plow passed and cut through the park where birch branches creaked and swayed in an ancient dance amidst the breeze. Her shadow was lengthened by the park lamps, and she quickened her pace on the path, skipping over puddles of slush and traversing a frosted storm drain with her long, Scandinavian legs. A gust of wind bounced off old city brick when she rounded the corner. She raised her wool scarf over her face, catching a tear that ran over her cheek bone.

Inside, she followed the low glow and murmur down the hall. The only lights were in the ceiling near the bar itself. They were dim and failed to reach most of the bistro tables, which were around the perimeter of the room. Each table had a small candle on its dark wooden top. The Cure played at a hushed volume from a vinyl record player on top of a stack of wooden crates. She ordered a house cabernet from a silent bartender and found Kristelena sitting near a window with a coat draped over her shoulders, almost drowning her tall, thin figure. Her hands were folded in her lap, right leg crossed over the left. She gazed out at passing traffic, following cars until they were out of sight and then starting again with the next one that came into frame. There was a kiss of lip stick on her wine glass. Turning to Sue, she wrinkled her notched chin and smiled between dark plum-colored lips.

"I hope you like this place. It's dingy, but it has character," Sue said. She set her stemmed wine glass down near the candle in the middle of the table and hung her coat and scarf on the delicate, aging bistro chair.

"It is a good place. Sort of...hipster?"

Sue agreed with a laugh. "It's our favorite little cafe, although there's not much to choose from in this town. It gets old sometimes, but places like this help."

"It's fun, thank you. We always have fun times with you and Michael."

"We are glad to show you around. I've never asked, have you been anywhere else in the US?"

"In the spring, we drove from New York to California in a rental car. The Redwood Forest was unbelievable, the best we have ever seen. It was scary, though. We got so...*xhai*? We smoked from our hash pen, got a little lost, and ended up surrounded by beers."

"Beers?"

"Yes, I show you." Kristelena slid her phone across the table and showed a video with a serene backdrop of Californian Redwood trees. The camera panned to a small, black bear. Another two appeared within seconds. Sue held her breath as one bear sprung from a seated position to four legs and ran straight towards the camera. Kristelena's worried face came into camera view and the video ended with hurried Russian speech and an up-close shot of the forest floor.

"Fortunately, no mama bear in sight," Kristlena said. She nodded with a hushed laugh. "It was the trip of a lifetime, even with the beers. We will definitely be traveling more. In Russia, you know, you do not live, you survive. This is the reason we want come here."

"Well, it sounds like you lived *and* survived your trip...so, when did you and Nikolai get married?"

"It's a long story. Really, I suppose the answer is January 2021, but we are not together, actually, and we did not intend to be married until we each decided to come to the US."

"What do you mean?" Sue asked. She had a nurse's warmth that showed when she asked probing questions. "So you wouldn't have gotten married if you didn't come here?"

Kristelena, perhaps anticipating Sue's questions, offered an explanation with complete confidence. "It's legal, but not true. The visa process was much easier for a married couple. To enter the lottery system as a married couple, we had a much better chance of getting here and staying. We have dated before, but we decided to get married before arriving here to better our chances. Also, it was easier for Gregory to hire us in this way."

Kristelena waited calmly for a response. She took her eyes off Sue and placed a finger on the base of her wine glass, anchoring it.

Sue gave a Minnesotan smile, burying any reaction that could be taken as judgment and instead offered understanding. "The visa process must be long and complicated. It must have been hard to leave friends and family behind. Do you miss them?"

Kristelena exhaled and lifted a finger from the base of her glass. "Yes, every day. We keep in touch through text message groups. They tell us how things are in Russia and elsewhere in Europe if they have left. You can't trust the news here or in Russia. It's always the same nationalism nonsense. People in Moscow see through Putin's bullshit, you know, but so much of the rural areas like him. He is very popular there...this such 'big man' and old KGB. Lots of people miss the Soviet Union. Everyone was more equal then, it is maybe true, but no one had much. Now, Putin owns everything. You can point your finger to anything on a map and he owns. It's a joke we play with each other. We look at the map or point to a nice house, and say, you see this? I heard Putin owns this."

Sue shook her head and peered out the window.

"What do you think of Russia?" Kristelena asked. She adjusted the coat on her shoulders while glancing around the room and placed her hands back in her lap.

"I think Putin is a dictator. It's not perfect here, either, but it seems much better," Sue said.

A draft swept across the floorboards as a group of twenty-somethings on an excursion from the college campus huddled inside. "I'm not just a communist, I'm a Marxist. Marxist philosophy is about economics and is still relevant," one of them asserted.

Another jested, "Well, my main point still stands: your beard makes you look like a communist and you should shave it."

Kristelena turned to Sue and rolled her eyes. "Oh please, I cannot escape. Not that it's possible."

3

"What can a bank argue to enforce its security interest in a T-note when a debtor defaults on their loan?"

Sitting beside a bubbling space heater, Michael struggled to comprehend this email subject line after reading it for a third time early Monday morning. As a second-year associate attorney at Brower & Wood, a medium-sized law firm nestled into the hillside in west Duluth, he was used to partner attorneys unloading obscure questions such as this one. Each time after failing to break ground, it led to fundamental questions about his choice of occupation. The doubts would simmer in the back of his mind until, as was always the case, he dug his way to answers through a combination of natural curiosity and black coffee.

The hours he spent researching these narrow questions benefited his billable hour requirement, which had increased to 1,900 hours in his second year. Lawyers in Chicago or Minneapolis worked more, but he was not practicing in either of these cities and was not paid as if he was working at that pace. His formal research memorandum would go out, and if he was lucky, the partner would send a note to at least confirm receipt.

The body of the email had no text. There was also no file

number to locate other correspondence for context. He ran an internet search for the term "T-Note" and clicked on anything with promise. "A treasury note," he whispered to himself in the blue light of the computer. "I'm sure there is plenty of caselaw on this. What kind of court would this even be in? A bankruptcy court?"

The watch on his wrist read seven a.m. He wore a vintage Longines Aviator Monday through Sunday. His uncle was a watch collector and gifted him the Longines after he graduated from law school. The inscription read: 'tick, tock—M.' The watch had to be wound by hand and, therefore, lost accuracy over the years, but it was typically within five minutes of the correct time. He enjoyed the black leather band, polished gold crown, and dark face with white numbering. His connection with the watch was emphasized by the sense that he had earned it.

In a gesture that was symbolic of his surrender, Michael tossed a ballpoint pen across his desk. It glided along the oak-top, stain resistant surface and tumbled onto the bristly, faded carpet below.

He wondered if he would ever possess the strength to resume. It would not be possible in any universe, he thought, without coffee, which required a trip through the firm's maze-like halls. And so he moved through the unlit, still firm as if the offices lining the walls were tombs and their mummies could be woken. Even with most offices on the outer walls, there was still no open space. The mid-section of the firm was disjointed: it was separated by legal assistants' cubes, two kitchenettes on opposite sides, a morbid law library, and several sterile conference rooms. Add to this, the lighting was not designed for such a layout, making it shadowed even when all the lights were on—they never were. The lake view was redeeming, notwithstanding that a heavily active shipyard and network of elevated, screechy train tracks drew the eye. But it was this shipyard that was Michael's favorite. Lake Superior's vessels intrigued him, and he often kept the harbor camera's live footage playing on one of his computer monitors as he worked.

The coffee machine gurgled, and Michael looked down the

narrow hall to the dark blue water, shipyard, and lead-colored sky. It was identical to the sky he'd seen three years prior outside the window of the US Embassy in Stockholm. As an intern with the US Department of State, he was permitted to work and study out of the Embassy while completing a law school term at Uppsala.

He was in the office of an American diplomat named Robert Hunt, who had agreed to discuss careers in the foreign service. Hunt's office was bigger than the others on the second floor, which was the highest Michael had security clearance to enter. An American flag stood in the corner with an affirming brass base, and a patriotic portrait of the founding fathers hung over the striped sofa where Michael sat, hands at his sides and feet planted on the navy blue carpet. Hunt sat across from him in an easy chair instead of behind the desk. He studied Michael's body language as if running down a list of possible signals. "Make yourself comfortable...you look... uncomfortable," Hunt had told him, offering to take his down winter parka.

"But sure, there's lots of lawyers who are FSOs or work in one of the Bureaus back in DC," Hunt had said. "I took the Foreign Service Officer Test right after the bar exam and never looked back. Of course, they sent me to New Delhi for the first two years. I got malaria and spent three months in a hospital bed my first year. You won't get to choose your first post. With a background in Russia and Eastern Europe, they might send you to a post-Soviet state like Armenia before sending you to the bigs in Moscow. Is that where you'd want to go? Moscow?"

"No, Russia is more of an academic interest for me. Does everyone who studies sharks have to swim with them?"

"The good ones do," Hunt had shrugged with a diplomatic and deferential smile.

Michael let the coffee finish brewing before taking a cup. There were some who claimed an imbalance in taste resulted if the coffee was poured too soon. He slipped back into his office and, until noon, researched caselaw, picking out court opinions, reading samples, and then casting them aside or filing them in a folder marked "File __".

At lunch, he found the sub sandwich marked with his name and embarked on the deceptively difficult task of finding a seat in the largest conference room. A seat too far away from the managing partner could make him appear unengaged or irrelevant, but a seat too close to the managing partner could upset more senior attorneys who were forced to move down the line or, worse, make him the first "volunteer" to write an article for the firm's website. Writing an article was not a billable task and, therefore, meant sacrificing a weekend. He found that one full-proof maneuver was to act like he was busy gathering documents or napkins for the table until more attorneys arrived and found their seats, leaving only one or two available, which usually landed somewhere in the middle.

Fortunately, Michael was no longer the rookie. Dalton Warth, a twenty-something with straight dark hair and a quiet manner recently joined the firm. Among other things, the Monday lunch meetings were a "welcome to the firm lunch." Like Michael, Dalton was also a graduate of the University of Minnesota Law School and was born and raised in Cloquet, Minnesota.

Dalton dressed formally for his first day, selecting a black suit with a black and red repp tie. Michael winced when he saw the black suit. Having been in the same position before, he anticipated the comments to come as he gathered napkins for the table.

John Sondheim, a senior partner already halfway through his sandwich, offered unsolicited but friendly advice. "We are outstate lawyers—we should be wearing tweed unless we're in front of someone in a robe, and even then, never wear a black suit because a jury, and probably even the judge, will think you're callous."

"Got it. I was on the fence about what to wear today," Dalton said too eagerly after John finished and before he could take another bite.

Offering his own opinion, Nate Patenaude, a young partner

with a fresh license to speak his own mind gave alternative advice by pointing out that John was the only attorney who wore a sport coat every day and that everyone else only dressed up for client meetings or court appearances. "It is true, though," Nate said in his shrill, confident voice, "you won't be as effective with the jury in a black suit." Addressing the whole room now, Nate shared on his last trial, "Opposing counsel—Taylor from Stoopleman who's been pretending to practice law for the last twenty years—wore the same black suit for the whole four-day trial. I don't think the jury liked him. He's also an asshole. Needless to say, the jury came back with $80,000 in compensatory damages in our favor. Did we not get any mayo with these?"

Macomber was a difficult file. There was no telling how late or in which direction the client meetings for it would go, and so Michael scheduled them for late in the afternoon. It was a matter he inherited from a departing associate, and he wondered if the file contributed to the associate's decision to leave the firm. Viewed in the most favorable of light, it simply involved revoking a power of attorney or convincing the client that revoking the power of attorney was unwise. It was unwise. In worse light, and probably a more honest one, the matter involved a sibling rivalry and rights to the family business.

All legal disputes involving families look the same from a distance. Michael's philosophy was that, up close, it didn't take long to uncover the unique qualities that distinguished them. Tolstoy famously suggested that all happy families are alike and each unhappy family is unhappy in its own way. The happy families made it look simple, even if a family business was involved. There were many ways for it to go wrong: divorce or a death forces family members to choose a side; tradition is lost through the sale of a family cabin or children move far away; all the children stay, but only one is chosen to take over a family business. Michael's client, Samuel Macomber, was chosen. As the oldest of the boys, he was always slated to take over the welding supply shop in west Duluth.

Pulling up to the welding shop, Michael surveyed the snow-laden roofs and faded storefronts. The maroon paint on the last two letters of the sign had vanished, so the name read 'Macomber's Welding Supp.' Samuel's apartment was directly above it. Typically, the sink was clean, floors vacuumed, and counter organized with the mail in a neat pile in the corner. That things appeared in a good state was a mark against Samuel's story that he was being taken advantage of. After reviewing hundreds of bank transactions Samuel flagged as being only in the interest of his brother and attorney in fact, Mathew, Michael did not see a clear argument against the propriety of the transactions. As attorney in fact, Mathew was tasked with buying groceries, essentials, and keeping up the apartment where Samuel lived. He was also the de facto manager of the welding shop. Contrary to Samuel's suggestions, the place was not in shambles, and the shop appeared to be operating. That the apartment was well-kept in the midst of a dispute suggested that Samuel was not being fully transparent about his treatment, especially where Mathew insisted that he was doing everything he could for Samuel. Mathew also accused Brower & Wood of trying to drain Samuel of his savings, which added pressure to matters.

It was difficult, though, *not* to believe a man confined to a wheelchair and borderline cognitive capacity. However, Michael's frustrations built as time progressed. And to Mathew's point, he thought the worst part was trying to balance his advocacy with the feeling that legal bills were eating up far too much of Samuel's savings for a pointless cause. This wasn't a job for a lawyer billing at several hundred dollars an hour, bound to serve at the direction of one party. It was a job for a family counselor or a social worker. He fielded call after call of complaints about things that, after carefully reviewing transactions and having conversations with Samuel, were verifiably false or contradictory.

Michael's notebooks were filled with inconsistent recollections. One week, Samuel would advise that he initiated and organized a roof replacement of the machine shed that cost thousands, speaking in detail about his communications with the contractor. The next week, he would suggest that Mathew orchestrated the roof replacement because he was anticipating Samuel's death and wanted to sell the property as soon as possible. Regardless of truth, any case against Mathew would be problematic because Samuel would not be able to tell a jury a consistent story. Michael, to himself, repeated the advice of an attorney who retired a month earlier: "The key task of the jury in a trial, Michael, is to decide who is lying and who is telling the truth. The *truth* is whatever they are convinced it is."

One step at a time, Michael thought to himself. He crunched over the snowy driveway in his brown Red Wing boots, which failed to absorb moisture because it was too cold for the snow to melt. A knock at the door went unanswered. A second knock was followed by noisy movement and a click of the deadbolt that was installed halfway up the door frame. After waiting a moment for Samuel to clear, Michael stepped into a living room filled with smoke and smelling of menthol cigarettes.

"What? You don't like smoke?" Samuel asked.

"I don't need one right now, thank you, though," Michael said. He pulled out documents from the file and placed them on the table. "Samuel, I wanted to talk to you today so we could clarify your position on these transactions. I'm going to walk you through all of these, and I want you to write down beside each one whether it is a transaction that you disagree with."

Samuel carefully reviewed and made notes by transactions in a shaky hand as Michael slid a magnifying glass down the list, leaning over on the edge of his seat.

The objective was reached within thirty minutes, and Michael lent a friendly ear for the next hour and a half. They had taken another step in the case, which was perhaps not a step closer, but at least a step further.

A bar called the Engine Room was the nearest warm place to compose a memorandum to the file while the information was still fresh. It was one hundred yards from an abandoned railway line. The interior of the Engine Room was covered with wood paneling and sprinkled with dusty taxidermy. The tin ceiling was painted scarlet and gave the room a reddish hue. There were two bar counters in the center of the room that faced each other and pointed down towards a narrow stage with faded black curtains. A slim, aged bartender with a grazing deer on his belt buckle shuffled up and down the back bar mixing drinks, taking cash, and emptying out glasses. He did all of this with expert precision while asking patrons about work and warning of incoming weather. It was too busy for just after four o'clock on a Monday afternoon.

Michael ordered a club soda and found a table in the back near the empty stage. Drafting a memorandum to the file took half the time if it was composed immediately after the meeting. After today's meeting with Samuel, it took just fifteen minutes. He checked the Longines, closed the file for the day, and bought a local dark lager.

The back of the bar was quiet, but a tall musician with a beard and black bandana wrapped around his wrist gently unpacked his guitar. Placing a bar stool in front of the microphone, he took a seat and announced himself informally to the few people listening as Nate Boots. He filled the room with a somber melody, and in a uniquely tender and earnest voice, sang: "Lost dreams in the wee hours, a ghost's kiss on the lips, paper heart, paper love, paper trust, papers ripped...shift shape like the shadows that descend and alight...in Sleepy Eye."

Trust and truth, Michael thought, are two distinct concepts. You do not necessarily need the truth to get someone to believe or act a certain way, but you need trust.

. . .

There were four cars left in the lot of the mostly deserted law firm. One was the cleaning crew's van and the other three belonged to attorneys, who were likely having post-work drinks in Sondheim's office. Before walking inside, Michael put together a simple plan to minimize the chances of getting roped into staying. He would not use the bathroom, which was near Sondheim's office. He would walk directly to the filing cabinets to return the physical file to its slot amongst the other large brown folders and stop quickly at his office to plug in his laptop for the night. He never took his laptop or files home.

The skinny silver key unlatched the staff door. Without turning on a light, his feet led him by muscle memory left at the kitchenette toward the file cabinet, where he quietly replaced the file and slid the steel cabinet inwards. His office was directly around the corner. With a satisfying magnetic click, he connected his laptop to the charger in his office. Coming back through the hallway near the kitchenette, he spotted John Sondheim pouring a glass of water from the cooler and said goodnight as he passed.

"Hey, Michael. Actually..." Sondheim said. He took a long pull from his glass.

Michael stopped and backtracked to the kitchenette. His throat tightened.

"I just wanted to let you know that the partners are happy with your work, so well done. Also, I wanted to say that, now that the firm has Dalton, you will probably get fewer research projects and will be taking on more client files yourself. You should start trying to develop your own book of business, but there's no rush."

"Does that mean within a year or within the next few months?"

"Probably months. I hope that Macomber file with those brothers and that rickety welding shop is going okay, I know that client has been difficult for a while. I'm not sure why we took that on to begin with."

"Seems like that happens once in a while. I don't mind. We all get one eventually."

Sondheim's words replayed in Michael's head as he walked to his car. He turned the ignition on and left the radio off. Before pulling out of the parking lot, he dialed Sue and transferred the audio to the car speakers.

"The last thing I want are more files like Macomber. If I'm not able to fill my billable time with research projects, I'll have to make up that time somewhere, and partners will throw God knows what my way if I'm not billing enough time."

"Do they have a specific area they want you to focus on?" Sue asked.

"As long as I'm billing, I don't think it really matters what type of work it is. No one checks."

4

For the remainder of the week, Michael spent as many hours as he could justify on research assignments and returned home early, rationing the work. He spent the weekend thinking of opportunities to recruit clients. He hit dead ends. Over dinner on Sunday in the apartment, Sue suggested that he attend local networking events or start reaching out to business people they knew from the area.

"I'm trying to get clients quickly, before getting assigned to three more 'Macombers,'" Michael said. He stacked their plates and brought them to the kitchen, scraping each into the trash.

"Nikolai and Kristelena may need help with their visas," Sue said. "Why don't you ask if they do?"

"If I had any idea how immigration law worked," Michael replied, "I would offer to help them."

"Can't you just read about it and figure it out. Isn't that what you do every day?" Sue came to the kitchen and placed a hand on Michael's back as he rinsed the plates. She took them and placed them in the dishwasher.

"Immigration is a specialized area, but it could be worth a

shot...I think we have an immigration attorney on staff if things were to get overly complicated."

"Or you could help them with a divorce," Sue said as Michael wrung out a dish cloth.

"No thanks, but why do you say that?"

"Did you know they aren't actually married?"

"No."

"Nikolai hasn't said anything about that?"

"He barely talks about Kristelena. What do you mean they aren't actually married?"

"Well, apparently, it's legal but not true, as Kristelena oddly explained to me. She told me that they just decided to get married for immigration reasons. I guess it was easier to get in the country if they were married. I thought something seemed off about them, about their relationship I mean, because it doesn't seem like they are romantic with each other."

"Isn't that similar to when people do green card marriages? I don't blame them for wanting to get out of Russia, either. Maybe they were nervous to tell us before," Michael said.

"Agreed, but still, I thought I would tell you. I don't really trust them, and not just because of the marriage thing. I never have. They've always seemed like they were giving part of the story. This is one example of that."

Michael paused. "I've felt the same, but I can't point to anything specific other than the marriage now. I have to go pick up Nikolai. Are you going out with Kristelena again?"

"She's picking me up soon. We're going to the Wine Bar. I think she likes it there."

Michael took a water bottle from the fridge. "I'll see you after the game tonight."

"Good luck and maybe don't ask Nikolai if they want to work with you."

Sue followed Michael out to the living room, kissed him goodbye, and turned on an Iggy Pop album. As she picked out her clothes from the bedroom closet, she thought about previous encounters with Nikolai and Kristelena. When the four were together, Nikolai and Kristelena asked Michael many questions. When Michael was away, they often asked questions about Michael. It was better to spend time with just Kristelena, she thought, because the conversations didn't revolve around him as frequently. The conversations between the two of them made Sue feel that she wasn't boring or difficult to speak with. Michael was able to transition between Russian and English, but they proved able to get along exclusively in English.

Seeing headlights through the blinds, Sue turned to see the Volvo station wagon pulling in and made for the door. She braced for the cold, adjusting her mittens after she locked the door. The car's old heating system blasted with little to show for it. Kristelena offered her warm, close-lipped smile. "Wine Bar?"

The road to downtown started at the top of the hill and wound its way down through frosted bluffs to the industrial part of town, where the half concrete, half brick plants produced the most life of anything within sight with their smokestacks steaming and workers coming, going, loitering.

Opening the old Volvo doors was made even creakier by the minus-three-degrees temperature. While preparing again for the cold and getting ready to make a dash for the entrance, Sue's phone slipped from her parka-coat pocket and found its way under the seat. She felt for it as she knelt outside the car. Her knee was singed by the permafrost ground. For a moment, she thought she felt a plastic phone case, but the shape was off. There were distinct ridges. Moving her hand to the left, her fingers finally brushed her phone screen, and she extended her fingers to extract it. But now there was a decision to make.

She hoped it wasn't what she thought, but she had the experience to know better. If it was anyone else, would she investigate? A nearby streetlight provided a weak beam. Kristelena could turn around any moment. She was twenty yards away, headed for the entrance in a hurry. Sue ducked back in.

A light, tentative grasp of the object confirmed her suspicion: Kristelena was driving with a handgun under the passenger seat. Sue knelt lower now and brought the gun under the glow of the streetlight, allowing the cold, hard plastic handle to rest in the palm of her hand as the wind picked up from behind her and an icy sweat formed on her lower back. The gun slipped easily from her hand back under the seat, as if she were dropping it into a body of water, hoping to never see it again. She shut the door, wrapped her face in her scarf, and ran ahead.

Kristelena slowed at the entrance with an unlit cigarette behind her ear and her hands in the pockets of her knee-length overcoat. Her head was down, and her black hair fluttered against the wind. She put the cigarette between her lips and brushed her hair back with one hand. "I'll meet you inside, Sue."

"I'll find us a table," Sue said. Her voice was steady as she moved past Kristelena through the steel door.

Across the street, steam rolled out from the concrete plant and interspersed utility lights shined brightly on patches of the surrounding sidewalk. A figure appeared walking between shadows, head leaning over feet. He moved with a measured gait towards Kristelena. They made eye contact for a moment before the man lowered his gaze. He wore a black denim coat with a newspaper tucked under one arm. He was in his late thirties. Lean face. Kristelena held her eyes on him until he came to the door, where they made eye contact again.

"Do you have a light?" he asked.

"Sure, it's no problem."

A freight train screeched to a stop at a nearby depot as he bent into Kristelena's flame. He gave her a quick thanks and asked if she was from the area. Kristelena, reluctantly, said she wasn't but that she came for a job as a dental assistant.

"Staying here for good?" he asked.

"Maybe. Probably not."

"You might want to find somewhere warmer than here. Sounds like you might be from somewhere cold, though, anyway."

"It's true, I am used to it." Kristelena laughed. It was soft and illusive. There was a palpable distance between her and the experiences that seemed to reel like old films behind her hazel eyes. It was as if it were a previous life, the scars of which were still imprinted on her consciousness.

"Me, too, I've lived here for a few years and Canada before that, which was even colder than here."

"So you are also not American?" Kristelena asked.

"No. I came here because the pay is better than in Manitoba for the same work."

Kristelena nodded with approval and put her cigarette in the outdoor ashtray. She introduced herself in clear English. The Canadian held out his hand, which was warm but dry and textured like a rug. He had thick black hair and the look of experience.

"Are you coming inside?" The man rubbed his hands together for warmth. It sounded like fabrics chafing against each other.

It reminded Kristelena of her father's electrician hands. It had been twenty years since she saw him last. "Many live a life of struggle," she heard him saying now, "if you must struggle, make it count. Make it on your own terms."

Sue looked with curiosity towards the bar and then back to Kristelena.

"I think cross-word Dan just wrote your name on the drink board," she said.

"What?"

"See that chalk board over there? You can buy someone a drink and write their name down for them to collect it. I think that guy just wrote your name down. Do you know him?"

"Yes, I just met him outside. He said his name was Mark. You call him curse-word Dan? Why?"

"Cross-word Dan. It's kind of a long story. Well, not really. There's a lot of people named Dan that come here, so Michael and I just give every guy who we don't know that name. As for the cross-word, check it out."

Following the direction of Sue's nod, Kristelena saw the bar where Mark was busy with his newspaper crossword. "He does that every time he comes here. What did you guys talk about?"

"I let him use my lighter and we talked a little. I like him. He looks like Joe Strummer."

"Is that your type?"

"He's a little too skinny for me, but I like his hands. How is work?"

"You know, it's Duluth. All the patients are super nice for the most part. Some of them even know my family or I know their niece or something. Other than that, it's a lot of drug-related incidents."

How dangerous could Kristelena be? Sue asked herself. Did she want to know more? Just pretend something came up and leave. Leave it behind. Leave it under the seat. But was Kristelena even aware? They sat silently, leaned back in their chairs. Kristelena, cross legged, dangled her foot, her toe pointed in Mark's direction.

"Should I go over there, Sue?"

No response.

"He could be fun," Kristelena said. She raised her eyebrows and looked in Mark's direction again.

Sue crossed her arms and leaned on her elbows. "Kristelena, did you know you have a gun under the car seat?"

Kristelena sighed and adjusted in her seat, no longer dangling a playful foot. "You know, foot flirting is an art form."

"I think you heard me," Sue said.

"It can be explained." Kristelena offered after a moment. Drawing in a breath now and lowering her gaze to the table, she spoke in a hushed tone. "You know how dangerous it is in this country, so people carry weapons? Dangerous for all. For us, for me and Nikolai, it is different. There could be random threats here, yes. But we have a more...specific threat. People from Russia could find us and try to hurt us, or they make someone else hurt us. It would be easy for them to make us disappear. That's why we ask the many questions of Michael. He speaks Russian. Why? I will tell you, we were more suspicious of you than you were suspicious of us when we met. It seemed too easy. A nice couple with money and a knowledge of Russian language and culture live in Duluth and want to be our friends? Take us out for dinner? Why? We thought you might be hired to gather information about us or make us disappear. Now we trust you, but there could be others. Listen to me...there *are* others. So, yes, I have fucking gun in car."

Sue sat quietly with her hands folded together on the table. She nodded slowly as she thought up a response. "We thought the same of you. We still don't know if we trust you. We feel like you aren't telling us everything, and maybe that's for the best."

"I think it is correct," Kristelena said. "But you feel we are the same, yes? Why else would you still be spending time with us? We have the same values and frustration with Putin's Russia...the kleptocracy...the nationalism. This is why we trust each other in ultimate case."

"So you are against the war?" Sue asked.

"Of course." Kristelena brushed her hair back, her serious hazel eyes fixed on Sue.

"Are you worried because of the protesting you did in Moscow before you left Russia?" Sue asked.

"Yes, many of our friends were arrested. This is one reason, but there are other things. Believe me, we are on the right side, the side that the West wants to win. This war is insane, and no one reasonable understands this. It is like you going to Wisconsin and start killing people. But Putin wants this land."

Unlocking her phone, Kristelena pulled up a map of Russia. "This is Putin's." Now, she pointed to Moscow. "This is Putin's." Then to St. Petersburg. "This is Putin's." She set her phone down and lifted her right elbow onto the table, resting her chin in her open right hand. With her fingers masking her lips, she leaned in and added, "This is not Russia. It is house of Putin and is shit."

5

The car door opened to Nikolai's grin and a dry snow flurry. Like driving, Michael and Nikolai took turns on control of the music. "I have a good album for tonight," Nikolai said. "This is classic rock, Michael. I don't expect you to know of this."

"Of course, I know Rush," Michael said. "This is better than that electronic stuff you usually play. My bus driver was obsessed with Rush in junior."

The heavy guitar of Rush's "Working Man" filled the car as they drove down side streets, over train tracks, and passed a man smoking a cigarette while riding his bicycle up the hill in the opposite direction.

"You played junior in Montana?" Nikolai asked. It was more of a statement.

"Yes, how'd you know?"

"I saw online. Good league?"

"Decent. Tough players."

"You had the same bus driver for all your trips?"

"Yeah. Dave. He was one of those guys that lived most of his life on the road. I think he drove freight most of his career before taking the job as our driver in his retirement. He had some crazy stories."

"Like what?"

"A lot of them were about sleeping at rest stops and seeing some things. He would warn us about lot lizards coming out at rest stops during the night, basically prostitutes making a pitch to drivers who were sleeping in their cabs. They'd come and knock on drivers' doors. Apparently, there was a driver once who didn't pay after accepting the company. The pimp came to the guy's truck, dragged him out of the cabin, and beat him up with one of those windshield squeegees that are next to gas pumps. Made me keep an eye out at those kinds of places for sketchy stuff."

"Lot lizards! I am learning good English words from you, Michael. In Russia, someone would probably get more than beat up if they tried something like that. It would have been fun for me to play over here. Were there lots of international players?"

"We did have some Russian and Ukrainian players. Most of the imports were from Scandinavia. You would have had a blast. We had one Ukrainian guy that was a brutal roommate on road trips. He would wake up yelling in Ukrainian during the middle of the night. He went back to Kyiv after the season in 2014 when Russia invaded Crimea. I've tried to look him up to see where he's at, to see if he's back home, hopefully still alive."

Nikolai paused for a moment and looked out the window. "I hope he's good. A lot of the guys there are in the military now. He maybe was not of conscription age back then but probably would be now."

"Did you ever think about going into the military?" Michael asked.

"Hell no, for what? For Putin? They have all these billboards and advertisements to make it look cool. No one in Moscow really goes for it. The military usually has to recruit from the smaller towns outside of Moscow or prisons. They take all the men from small towns, so people in Moscow don't even realize how bad the war is; it's not their men going. A lot of my friends who went to university and lived in Moscow left once the war started. A lot of them went to Kazakhstan and had to leave their stuff behind, just packed their cars with what they could and left. They all worried... like me...that the military would start coming for us. Probably better here than in Kazakhstan. I got lucky. Kazakhstan is cheaper, though."

Pulling into the parking lot, Nikolai scanned the cars. "So many trucks, Michael, why don't you drive one?"

"I should. I think they're all sold out though by the looks of it. Maybe you should try to get one."

"It is my dream. I want one of the big ones with the big pipe in the back."

"An exhaust pipe?"

"Exactly. I will drive this and pretend I am your friend Dave."

The dressing room was lively. "Nicky sweet hands," Paul said, as Nikolai and Michael set their bags down and began to retape their sticks. "I have to get a copy of your citizenship papers for the league."

"I don't have citizenship. What's the problem?"

"Relax, I'm just kidding. No one cares. By the way, I did forge your signature on the waiver of liability form. That's for real. I did that for everyone, though. Don't sue me, Mike."

"If I lose any more of my teeth, I'm coming after you for the best set of jibs money can buy, maybe even implants," Michael said. He was missing two of his front teeth, which were knocked out during a hockey game when he was nineteen. The false teeth he used daily made his smile look real. He often took the false teeth out and placed them in friends' beer glasses when they weren't looking, which was always to Sue's dismay. Michael said, "People think they'll look cool if they lose their teeth, but it looks ridiculous anywhere outside the hockey rink." His false teeth were out, and he emphasized the lisp on 'ridiculous' through his gaps.

"And if I get hit," Nikolai added, "Michael is going to sue you so that I can drive the biggest truck in the lot."

"If you score tonight, I'll buy you a trucker hat," Michael said. "Kristelena will love it."

"Maybe. What is a trucker hat?"

"You'll know when you see it," Michael said.

As the game progressed, the opposing team grew frustrated with trying to contain Nikolai. He was dominant. In the corner, he came away with the puck. Through the middle, he was untouchable. Around the net, anything off his stick went in. Players slashed and tripped. He danced around them.

At the start of the third period, Nikolai retrieved the puck off the side boards, skated ahead, and chipped the puck behind the defense at the blue line in front of the team bench. The defenseman stretched his leg out so that he collided with Nikolai, knee against knee. Nikolai fell to the ice. Michael, instinctually, leapt from the bench.

"You and me," Michael said as he approached the offending player, who had already started skating to Michael with a welcoming smile underneath a patchy beard. They latched onto each other's jerseys and held steady with one hand. Blows were exchanged as they twisted in a circle. Punches landed on chins and cheek bones, fists cracked the top of helmets, until, exhausted, they clutched shoulders, pinning arms down. Both teams rattled the bench boards in acknowledgement. The referee separated them, saying, "Jesus Christ, it's Sunday night, boys. I had my hand up already, Michael." A gash under Michael's eye dripped blood onto the milk-white ice below. He wiped his face with his damp jersey and scattered the frozen blood by skimming his skate blade across the ice.

As Nikolai untied his skates after the game, he leaned over to Michael and thanked him for stepping in. "I owe you now, don't I?"

"It's no problem, that was a cheap shot. That guy was out of control and needed one." Michael slid the snow from his skate blade onto the black rubber floor below. "He was doing that stuff all game. I told myself I'd fight him if it escalated."

"How's business going for you?"

"Pretty slow. Know anyone that needs a lawyer?"

"Actually, I have a friend who I think could use your help. He has money, too, and maybe you could take him on as a client."

"What's his story?"

"He's a friend of Gregory's. His name is Alexei Stakhanovich, and he owns a small manufacturing business. He is Ukrainian."

"Does he need help with a lawsuit or a transaction?"

"Not a lawsuit, a transaction, I think a sale of some goods."

"Good, I don't like litigation. I might be able to help out with a sale."

"You should come see him tomorrow. I will come to introduce you. Maybe we can meet for lunch near his business."

Michael was intrigued. If Alexei really had some money and Michael established himself as his lawyer, he could be a steady source of income for the firm and give Michael some control over his billable time. With luck, the transaction could lead to Michael serving as Alexei's primary lawyer for negotiations. He explained all this to Sue in the living room when he got home, still smelling of hockey, dried blood on the cut below his eye.

"What happened to your face?"

"Someone gave Nikolai a cheap shot and we got in a bit of a tilt."

"Seriously, Michael? It doesn't matter who started it. You are twenty-seven years old. You don't need to be getting into fights over some cheap shot in your beer league. It's not worth it. Don't fight anymore, okay? Let the referees do their job. There's an ice pack in the freezer. I'll get a cloth."

"What do you think about the client meeting?" Michael asked, his head inside the freezer. It cooled his face.

"I think that's great, Michael. I agree this really could be something beneficial. It's just...I need to tell you more about Kristelena and Nikolai." She took the ice pack from him and wrapped it in the cloth. "Everything is okay, and I think there is a rationale behind this, but it was shocking. We got to the Wine Bar, and I found a gun under Kristelena's seat."

"Are you serious? What kind of gun?"

"A handgun. I've seen the kind before. I'm almost positive it was a Glock 18."

"Is that a pretty serious gun?"

"It's a fully automatic 9-millimeter machine pistol, so yeah."

"Is that even legal to have?"

"I think there are a lot of restrictions. My neighbor took me and my dad shooting once and he had one, but he's a state trooper. I think it's technically considered a machine gun."

"Did you ask her about it?"

"We talked about it. She explained that it's for self-defense and that they are worried people might try to hurt them. People from Russia who aren't happy with them. They're very anti-Putin, and I think they're worried about someone coming after them for political reasons. Remember them telling us about when they protested in Moscow? They sold all their things and left in a hurry after that."

"It seems like there would be a remote chance of anything happening to them in the United States. Did she say where she got it from?"

"She didn't think it was that remote of a chance. She didn't say where she got it from. I told her we're not sure if we trust them and that we feel like they aren't telling us their whole story."

"That's the honest truth. What did she say?"

"That they were suspicious of us when we first met because we were friendly and you spoke Russian. It seemed too easy, and they were worried you might be trying to get information from them or get them in trouble. That's why they ask you so many questions. She said that we have the same underlying values, though, and that they are on the right side of all of this."

"Trying to get information? We haven't asked them anything

deep about their lives. They volunteered their story within two hours of meeting. The protests in Moscow, selling their cars and flat, moving and not looking back. Also, do you remember when we first started playing tennis with them? I spoke a bit of Russian to them when I overheard, but they kept the conversation alive and invited us to play doubles. Then they messaged us almost every other day until we set up a recurring game. I remember it was exhausting trying to respond to them. They were eager, so I'm not sure why Kristelena said they were suspicious. They do ask me a lot of questions, but I don't know if it's because they're scared."

"Are you still going to go to the meeting tomorrow? Maybe we shouldn't be getting more involved with them," Sue said. She crossed her arms and moved to the doorway, leaning forward against the door frame in a way Michael had not seen before. She tapped her fingers nervously on her elbow.

"I'll still go, and I won't take the matter on if it doesn't feel right, okay? I think they just need a lawyer to negotiate and look a contract over."

"I don't like it. They have guns. I'm picturing you in the back of some warehouse making a deal with suspicious crates all around like in the movies."

"Nikolai texted me when I got home. It's far from a warehouse. Looks like the meeting will be at Collette's."

"Fancy. At least you'll be well fed. Promise you'll leave if it's weird?"

"I'll leave if it seems like something I can't handle."

Michael left the next morning long before the winter sun rose. The words from Boots' song were suddenly swirling around in his head. "Paper love and paper trust shifting shape like shadows." *And I'm standing right in the middle of it, with just enough light to see shadows,* Michael thought, warmth collecting in his stomach.

At the firm, he went through his routine, arriving early and moving around corners delicately like a thief trying to avoid detection. It was unnatural. But now more than ever, he did not want to get pulled into an unwanted assignment. He knew the one he wanted.

Michael was in Sweden again as his coffee brewed in the dimly lit kitchenette, the fire-orange bulb of the machine staring back at him. He was on the ferry from the mainland port at Nynäshamn on his way to the Swedish island of Gotland, where he would study for exams and walk the medieval walls of Visby. He sat at a high-top table next to large windows in the ferry canteen. It was late 2019, and as part of his duties as an intern with the State Department, he was reviewing the deposition testimony of Fiona Hill, compiling a timeline of events for the Bureau of Legislative Affairs in connection with the impeachment inquiry of President Trump and Ukraine relations. The Russian exclave and military base of Kaliningrad was only two hundred miles away. He was the only patron in the canteen. "Have you ever seen a Russian submarine out here?" he remembered asking the cashier.

"I probably have and didn't know it," the young Swede said.

"Kaliningrad is not far, right?"

"Not far, not fun. Makes us nervous, especially with things below, like fiber optic cables and pipelines. That's why Sweden is bringing more military to Gotland. The island has been important for the military historically, but not so much as long as I've lived here, or since my parents have lived here actually. The Russians started with Crimea, and everyone in Europe is watching closely for what happens next."

Paper coffee cup in hand, Michael returned to his office, gently closed the door, and flipped on a lamp. He searched for the name "Alexei Stakhanovich" on the internet and found nothing. It wasn't uncommon in dealing with local business people, whose businesses may or may not have a web presence.

But why Collette's? It was an obscure French restaurant on the side of a highway far south of Duluth. What he knew was that it had fantastic food, ghastly décor, and it was extremely under the radar. Discreet.

He gritted his way through other chores over the next several hours and emerged to a shared legal assistant's desk. Katherine was in her fifties, kind, and had been with the firm since she was in her twenties. She had that authority which comes from knowing the firm's internal politics, and Michael frequently consulted her in trying to navigate the landscape. She also helped with filings, drafting letters, and vetting new clients. She had blackish, grey hair and thin-framed glasses. She seemed to never blink under the thick lenses.

"Katherine, could you run a conflict of interest check on the name Alexei Stakhanovich?"

Michael handed her a post-it note with what he thought would be the correct spelling. "I'm not sure what his business is called yet or who the adverse party would be, but I'll send you a note later."

"Sure. I'll try this spelling in the system and a couple of others. What happened to your face?"

"Hockey game, does it look bad?"

Katherine winced. "It looks like it hurts."

"It feels okay."

"Are you going out for lunch?" she asked, noticing that Michael had his coat and work bag.

"Yes, I'll probably be back around two. I'm going to Collette's for a client meeting. Can I bring you back anything?"

"No, thank you. But you should try their chicken wellington. That's my favorite dish there."

"I will give it a try. Thanks, Katherine."

"And, Michael, maybe don't wear the Carhartt with the new client?"

"I'll change into the overcoat in the car. If you find anything on Alexei, just email me and I'll take a look before the meeting."

Back in the cold, the Red Wing boots crunched once again on the icy ground. He rolled the Carhartt up into a ball and threw it into the back seat, where he found no overcoat. He put the Carhartt back on. He liked it more anyway.

6

Collete's parking lot, down an access road and opposite a gas station, contained Nikolai's Volvo and a brown Mercedes sedan that appeared to be from the early 2000s. The glass door was lighter than Michael expected and burst open. Nikolai and two other Eastern European men were sitting at a table in the main dining room. No other tables were occupied. Michael guessed that the man sitting at the head of the table between Nikolai and the other man was Alexei. He had dark hair, a round face, and wore a navy-blue crew neck sweater with a silver watch. The third man had short grey hair and wore a tight, thinly striped button-down shirt.

"Michael, hello!" Nikolai said, rising from his seat. There were water and wine glasses at each table setting. Two bottles of wine were placed in the middle, both red. Nikolai's acquaintances also rose from their seats, both serious.

"Very glad to meet you, Michael. Come, enjoy some decadence," Alexei said. He had a deep, raspy voice and a warm smile that matched his rounded face. His cologne smelled of black tea, mint, and wet cobblestones. "This is my associate, Oleg."

"Glad to meet you both," Michael said. His hand found the

tight, brief grip of each of theirs. "You wouldn't be able to tell from the highway, but this restaurant has very good food. I can already tell we are going to get along just fine." He hung the Carhartt on the chair.

"Of course. We have a factory site in this area, so we have come here many times. It is a nice quiet place. Now," Alexei began, "I'm not sure how much Nikolai has told you." Michael had the sense that Alexei knew exactly how much Nikolai had told him, which was nothing. "But before we begin, I just want to make sure we are on same page. You see, Michael, you are an attorney, yes?"

"Yes, I'm an attorney with the law firm of Brower & Wood."

"I see. You know, Nikolai is Russian. Oleg is also Russian. But I am Ukrainian. I come from Kyiv. You studied Russian in college, yes? *Vy govorite po-russky*?"

"I majored in Russian, but my language skills have suffered every year since I graduated. I also know a little Ukrainian from some old hockey teammates."

"Why did you decide to study Russian?"

"In 2014, just before I went to college, I was playing junior hockey out west and there were Ukrainian and Russian players on the team. The languages were interesting to me. Crimea was also invaded around then, and I spoke with my friends often about the conflict. It led me to studying Eastern Europe, not specifically Russia. The closest thing offered at my university to an Eastern European major was Russian, so I went with that."

"We remember 2014 and saw all the signs leading up to this," Nikolai said. Michael wondered what 'we' meant. "It was hard to miss in the news, but I saw it personally when I stayed with my cousins on the Black Sea in Crimea before the invasion. It was in front of our faces. We would go down to the water and see "Krym" and "Nash" imprinted all over the beach. This is understood in Russian as "Crimea" and "Ours." The Russian nationalist tourists wore flip flops with the words printed on the bottom of each shoe.

Then it became an internet meme popular with the nationalists. Now, to the...delight...of many, it's being used ironically by anti-imperialists to mock the dysfunction in Putin's Russia. My most favorite: "Our toilets don't work but at least Krymnash!"

"I have been friends with Nikolai's aunt and uncle since our school days," Alexei said. "There are many Russians like Nikolai with Ukrainian connections. This is why an invasion is...so absurd, actually. It would be as if Minnesota claims right to Canada and started shooting at those nice Canadians. Totally absurd, actually. Was it hard to pick up the Russian language?"

"At first, but I ended up doing well and earning a scholarship for it."

"But no formal Ukrainian?"

"No."

"That's okay, we can work more on your informal Ukrainian," Alexei offered with a wink. "And forgive me, I'm not so familiar with the American legal rules, but even if we do not engage you here today, my understanding is that attorney-client privilege is still present. Is this correct?"

He knows more than most clients it seems, Michael thought. "Yes, I wouldn't call it attorney-client privilege, per se, if you do not become a client, but I owe you a duty of confidentiality even if you do not engage me. I will keep the conversation confidential either way."

"This is axiomatic, I think, Michael," added Oleg, pursing his thin lips. His sharp blue eyes were fixed on Michael. "We cannot continue unless you can give us this assurance. We are relying on you."

Oleg didn't make a striking impression at first glance. His short grey hair, mild build, and quiet demeanor weren't threatening, but his eyes, now locked on Michael, were piercing and the atmosphere changed when he spoke, as if a bird had flown into a window and was struck dead on impact. Where Alexei communicated with a balanced combination of warmth and intelligence, Oleg made declarations with chilling effect.

More lawyerly now to match the tone, Michael said, "Of course, you can rely on me to keep this confidential. Could you give me just a brief description of exactly what you might need my assistance with?"

"Thank you, Michael. Well, we believe you have experience with sales, forming new business entities, and bank accounts. Is this correct?" Alexei asked.

"Yes, I have experience with all of those. What kind of sale are you doing?"

"It is sale of goods from my company, Minnesota Instruments, LLC, a company which I have recently purchased in my personal and sole capacity. The company makes safety valves for the industrial setting, and we have buyer lined up in Sweden for a sale of around $10 million."

"Sweden? I've had some experience there, but not as a business lawyer," Michael said.

"Yes, Nikolai has told us this," Alexei said.

"But congratulations on the sale," Michael said. I've helped some of our bigger manufacturing clients with a couple international transactions. To be honest, they haven't been that big, but still in the million-dollar range. The same principles should still apply."

"This sale is step one," Oleg said. "We will need a lawyer, a US lawyer, to help us navigate and negotiate terms and conditions of sale and payment."

"Understood. In similar situations, our seller typically uses a letter of credit to secure payment from the foreign buyer."

"Okay, and you could draft this letter of credit?" Alexei asked.

"Yes, and I would coordinate with your bank and the buyer's bank to see it through. It's a financial tool that would protect both parties. It will guarantee that you get paid. Basically, the letter will spell out what needs to happen in order for the sale to be deemed complete, such as the official export and import of the correct quantity of goods. Once the buyer's bank acknowledges that the goods are in the hands of the buyer, that bank will release payment to your bank. The letter is the buyer's bank's guarantee that payment will be made if the goods are provided, which is better than you just taking the buyer's word that payment will be received."

"Oleg is running the books. He can provide our banking details. It isn't a worry that the buyer does not have enough funds to make payment, but this is why we need a lawyer...to make sure we still have protection in case the buyer doesn't *want* to make payment for some reason. You have earned a glass of wine, Michael, and so have I." Alexei reached for a bottle of cabernet sauvignon.

As he did so, the waitress appeared and obligingly poured four glasses of wine. "Have we decided on lunch?" she asked, carefully pouring the wine and acknowledging Alexei at the head of the table.

"I will have petite filet with shrimp," Alexei said. Oleg ordered the same but clarified that the filet should be well done. Nikolai ordered the chateaubriand to be preceded by a salad. Not having looked at a menu, Michael opted for the chicken wellington.

"Our request does not end here, Michael," Alexei continued when the waitress was out of earshot. He leaned in now. "We want you to help us use the money from this sale in a meaningful way." Alexei sat back, swirled, smelled, and sipped his wine. It was as if he was back in Kyiv at a sidewalk café, listening to the chatter of his countrymen in the background.

He returned from this reminiscence with an expression of sincerity and gravity. His jaw fell lower. His eyes focused. Oleg and Nikolai remained motionless, absolutely silent.

"Nikolai says that you are sympathetic to what is happening in Ukraine. I believe your conversations in 2014 have something to do with this, as well as your studies. We believe, given the opportunity, you might be willing to make a difference with the plight of Ukraine and for the greater struggle against Putin's Russia. Tell me, what do you think of this?"

Michael paused, scanning their faces. "I am sympathetic to the Ukrainian cause, and I think Putin is a great danger to Europe, as well as the rest of the world. I'm not sure how I can make a difference in my position, but I'm willing to listen to anything you might have in mind and play whatever small part I can from my position as your lawyer and adviser. Are you thinking of some type of fundraising or donation? I would be glad to assist with that."

"This is very good news, Michael. This is very good, and we are glad to have been right about you. Are you sure you don't have Ukrainian blood? Fundraising is precisely what we have in mind." After reflecting, Alexei added, "It is somewhat complicated, however, because we do not intend to engage in what you would call traditional fundraising or donating. We do this because of all the bullshit and politics that surrounds aide to Ukraine. There is way to make...more direct impact. We want to be in control, and we will have the proper channels to distribute funds to where it is most needed. Now, Michael, you have seen on the news that Americans have gone to fight in Ukraine, yes?"

"I have seen that, yes," Michael said, his palms beginning to sweat. He took a sip of wine to slow things down, and the others waited patiently. He couldn't taste a thing.

"This is very good to have volunteers. Money and supplies can only get Ukraine so far. They need soldiers...but do you know what the problem is? We do not have enough volunteers and many of the volunteers are inexperienced. They arrive in Ukraine and do not have an idea of what to do. It creates difficulty for the Ukrainian military. It complicates things. We need soldiers with previous military experience. We need to make it easier for *experienced* soldiers to come fight, and we need the inexperienced ones to be trained. Of course, we aren't talking about setting up some terrorist style boot camp here in Minnesota. What we need to do is give resources and encouragement in support of specific missions. What if we could offer a $25,000 bonus or more to Americans with valuable military experience? This would be incredibly valuable for recruitment."

"I see where you are coming from, and I'm not sure if that's legal," Michael said.

"Right now, any American can walk into the Ukrainian Embassy in the United States and make commitment to Foreign Legion of the Territorial Defense of the Armed Forces of Ukraine. Americans can also engage Ukrainian recruiters on the Foreign Legion website, and someone will begin the recruitment process. These volunteers are even entitled to payment when they arrive in Ukraine, as well as bonus, but pay is very low for foreign recruits. All we are talking about here is 'sweetening the deal' as you say. It will save lives and potentially shorten the war."

"How do you imagine this type of distribution to volunteers happening?" Michael asked.

"We are not asking you, Michael, whether this is ultimately legal," Oleg said. "We are giving you this background so that you might be more willing to help in your capacity as our lawyer and so that you are not surprised...to see what happens. We tell you this because of trust. We have other people working out how distributions will happen. We want you to feel like you are making a difference and not as if we are hiding our agenda."

"All we need you to do, Michael, is negotiate our contract, potentially more to come from Scandinavia, and, as a step two, establish a few companies and bank accounts to distance my company from the distributions," Alexei said. "I don't want my American company directly tied to funding this effort."

"Alexei is the sole owner of the LLC. He may take a member withdrawal, the proper way, and then transfer funds through channels separately. It will all be proper," Oleg said.

The food arrived. As wine glasses were refilled, Michael was allowed to absorb the proposal as they quietly started their dishes. The red wine and hearty plates produced a sense of comfort and homeyness. They were all at a sidewalk cafe in Kyiv now. They were citizens of the world. Michael turned the request over in his head, changing perspectives, playing hypotheticals, all with the hope of concluding that any caution could be thrown to the wind, and in a way, the potential hazards making it seem an even more significant way to make an impact.

"Do you have an accountant?" Michael asked.

"Oleg does our books and is excellent with accounting," Alexei said.

"If anything, I could help with the legal side of the sales transaction and forming new companies, but you'll need an accountant for dealing with the actual cash flow."

"Of course, we work together, but we will need your expertise to complete this sale and properly organize the new businesses. This is a new company for me, and they have never handled a sale this large, nor an international sale. They usually do not negotiate contract terms. Instead, they just accept a purchase order, send the goods, and collect the money. It is more complicated in this case because the buyer wants special written agreement on the terms and conditions, and we want to make sure it is a done deal, no loopholes."

"I will think about it," Michael offered.

"This is all we ask at this point, Michael," Alexei said. "As for your fee, Michael, we are willing to offer you a retainer fee for the work you will put in. What is your hourly rate?"

"My rate is $350 per hour. A retainer isn't necessary but would help me justify this matter as a priority to the firm."

"Michael, if you will agree to represent us, we will offer you a retainer of $50,000, more if it helps. If you do not bill up to this point, return the remainder of money to us. We will come back to Collete's for dinner, and we will give you the rest in cash personally."

"Thank you, but that won't be necessary. I will take you up on the dinner, though. Before we go further, I will do a conflict-of-interest check at the firm to make sure everything is squared away. I don't imagine we've represented the Swedish buyer, but please still send me their details and any other background information." *Anything to buy some time*, he thought.

Handing Michael a manilla folder, Alexei added, "Excellent. Thank you again for your interest in helping us. I think this could be a great partnership. Now, did you know, Michael, that this is one of the few restaurants outside of the Twin Cities that serves Dom Perignon?"

"I did not know that, but I think I will have to be getting back to the office actually. They'll get jealous if I'm out too late at a client lunch and try to steal you for themselves."

"Nonsense Michael, please stay for just one toast."

The Dom Perignon was presented at the table. Oleg set his glass aside while he rolled a cigarette, brushing the leftover tobacco onto the floor with the back of his hand. Dutifully, Michael stayed for Alexei's toast "to success." He tasted the champagne before placing the full glass back on the table. Finally, he made his goodbyes and requested that Nikolai walk with him out to his car. It was beginning to snow.

"Michael, I'm sorry we kind of surprised you with this, but it's really just the legal work they need from you. Alexei found it very difficult to get a lawyer he trusted. He wanted to work with you."

"Nikolai, are you telling me everything?"

"Michael, come on. I'm telling you all that is relevant, and I can try to help you. What do you want to know?"

"Is this sale for real?"

"Yes, of course."

"Why is there suddenly a Swedish buyer that is connected with the largest transaction this company has received? Do they know what Alexei plans to do with the proceeds?"

"Alexei had the connections to make the deal happen. Does it truly matter to you whether the buyer knows about where the proceeds are going? If it's not actually necessary, I don't think it's helpful for you to know. It's simple: the buyer is buying goods in exchange for money."

"Unless I'm aiding in something illegal, it's not really my place to inquire or judge on how the client spends their money. I'm not sure where this stands yet."

"Michael, you heard Alexei talk about Americans already fighting in Ukraine for the Foreign Legion. This is not illegal. I don't know how much the buyer knows. Once the sale is made, the money is out of their hands anyways, right?"

"When you came to the tennis court that day, did you have this request in mind?"

"No—we didn't have the details worked out yet. You have to understand, though, Michael, I'm a person of action. So is Kristelena, and so are the two you just met. The question is if you want to be a man of action or if you want to sit on the sidelines."

"Why haven't you brought any of this up before?"

"It wasn't the right time to bring you in yet."

"Bullshit, you should have told me," Michael said, walking away with his hands in his coat.

"Would you have agreed to meet with us today if I told you? Honestly?" Nikolai followed him, hands raised by his sides, his eyes concerned. "I don't think you would have, and I'm telling you about it now."

"What have you told Alexei and Oleg about me?"

"That you care, that you went to college to study Eastern Europe, and that you wouldn't be afraid to help us."

"Who are you? Ukrainian intelligence?"

"It's complicated. I will tell you more another time if you want to take this on."

"What about the gun in your car? I'm sure Kristelena told you about her conversation with Sue and the Glock she found under your seat. Are you carrying a gun around because of what's going on with Alexei?"

"Yes, and other things, but it's just a precaution. I thought you

Americans were okay with guns? Look, it's just for our protection. We don't know of anyone specific that is coming after us. We aren't on the run or anything like this. I think you already know, though, Michael, that this type of business can be dangerous and doesn't come without a certain amount of risk. I think we can do this sale and the recruitment project in a safe way and so do Alexei and Oleg. We are not selling arms here; we are only talking about selling legitimate goods and simply providing money to recruits...I will let you make your own decision."

"I'm not making any commitments right now. The smart thing to do would be to go back to my office and write up a letter declining representation. That's it."

"I know you are not going to do that, Michael. I think you are glad we asked you this today. Sidelines or action, it's your choice."

Alexei and Oleg appeared around the corner, stopping for a cigarette under the awning of Collete's. Alexei wore a tan mackintosh trench coat and flat, English cap. The snow fell harder and collected on the awning. As goodbye, Michael shook Nikolai's hand without another word, waved to the other two, and climbed into the car. Checking his phone as the car defrosted, an email from Katherine appeared:

To: Michael Lund

Re: The Stakhanovich Matter

From: Katherine Cornwell

Results: No Conflicts. No File Matches Found.

Potential Client Name: Alexei Stakhanovich

Adversary: N/A

Business: N/A

Michael reached for the folder containing the Swedish buyer's details. Produktion Group AB Stockholm was a steel manufacturer in Stockholm, Sweden. The company's contact details were listed, as well as the quotation for the sale from Alexei's company, which Michael did not wish to review in the parking lot as the others stood nearby. He drafted a quick reply to Katherine, asking her to check if the firm had ever been involved with Minnesota Instruments, LLC, and that she do an internet search on the Swedish manufacturer to see if they existed. As he exited the parking lot, Alexei shook his head in concern in response to something Oleg said. Oleg put both his hands on Alexei's shoulders, offered some words, and awkwardly gave his shoulders a pat.

7

From its website, Produktion Group AB Stockholm appeared to be a legitimate business, complete with a physical address, display of offerings, about page, and sales contact information. Katherine's report on Minnesota Instruments, LLC, showed that there were no previous matters in the firm's system involving the company, which meant no context from a previous file was available but also no history that might make the representation complicated, such as a representation in a messy lawsuit against the company.

"Go ahead and make a file for this, Katherine," Michael said. "Could you also send me our standard engagement letter with the retainer arrangement included?"

"Sure thing—congratulations on pulling in a client," Katherine said as she looked up from her desk through her thick lenses, probably knowing that Michael was under pressure to start generating business.

Michael left the lights turned off in his office and watched the snow falling silently outside the window from his desk. The flakes were heavy and wet, like little clouds tumbling from the sky. *Oleg gives me the creeps,* he thought.

If it weren't for Nikolai and Alexei, he would probably walk.

And Nikolai was right, he *was* glad that Alexei requested this assistance.

The request, at least as it was presented, made sense. They were relying on him to aid in making a real difference and to keep the matter confidential, to keep it secret. On this, his stomach suddenly got lighter, and he rested his elbows on his knees. What would happen if this arrangement was exposed? But what arrangement? The proposal was to negotiate a sale, possibly more to come, and then organize new business entities. Was the rest of it any consequence for the services that were requested? Movement in the corner of the window caught his eye. Someone was slowly crawling underneath the trees. *Well, that's it, I'm already burned*, Michael thought. *The waitress at Collete's was a spy. She called in her surveillance team to track me, and now they are coming to finish me.* Perhaps it was too small to be a person. He pressed his face against the cold window to track the figure around the corner: a large beaver dragging a log down to a nearby creek. He shook his head and scoffed at his own paranoia. *Think, one step at a time. Be logical, but don't be fucking scared.*

Isn't the just, courageous, and fair decision to support Alexei's effort? Alexei is a client like any other, and what he chooses to do with his money is up to him. In a broader sense, Ukrainians and all those who want to stop Putin's war have an interest in supporting Ukraine. The Swedes have an interest in ending Putin's aggression as well, even if the buyer doesn't know it. *If you're not up to it*, he thought to himself, *call the police and keep walking the line. Know your risk, then decide...identify the limitations and live with it, you know what is right. Nothing is truly stopping you, only the artificial.*

Taking the proposed legal services aside: was it legal for Americans to be paid to fight in Ukraine as Alexei suggested? Michael was not convinced. He switched the lamp on and turned to the computer to research like he had never done before.

Doubts subsided over the next few hours, as he devoured anything he could get his hands on that related to Americans voluntarily fighting in Ukraine, leading to the central point: American volunteers are paid for service once they arrive in Ukraine and sign the contract for service. As Alexei suggested, the pay was low. A bonus would certainly help. The web page for the Ukrainian Foreign Legion provided that volunteers get the standard pay of a Ukrainian soldier, varying depending on the conditions of the service. It was around $1,000 per month outside a dangerous zone, or up to $5,000 per month during combat deployment. There was also an option to join the Foreign Legion by signing up on the web page, as Alexei mentioned. The web page even had a chatbot to answer questions about recruitment, which Michael declined to engage after temptation.

But what would make it illegal? he thought to himself. He combed through legal journals, cross references, old cases, and news articles. "Section 959 of the Neutrality Act...prohibiting anyone within the United States from enlisting or paying someone else to enlist in a foreign military..." He read again, "*within the United States.*" Another source stated that "applicable law focused...on prohibiting efforts within the jurisdiction of the United States."

The problem, if prosecution was pursued, would be if Alexei actively recruited and paid Americans *in* the United States for service in Ukraine's military. If it was arranged so that the volunteers were formally enlisted and paid *after* they arrived in Ukraine, Alexei's plan could ultimately be defensible, if not completely valid. He could at least advise that recruitment efforts and payments be made outside the United States, including passive online recruiting from abroad. There was the open trail. Right in front of him.

But what the hell am I going to tell Sue, he thought as he quickly drafted the engagement letter for Alexei's signature, as if he would change his mind if he waited any longer. *I will tell her tonight, and she might understand. She has to understand.* Michael printed and signed the letter. He blew the ink dry, confirming his decision, and placed it in his desk drawer.

It was dark outside. The snow had stopped, but the three inches collected on the windowsill indicated a thick snow had fallen. Most of the lights were off inside the firm. Michael's watch read 6:10 p.m. The adrenaline was easing.

Michael shut down the computer and grabbed his Carhartt from the back of the chair. His hands were steady as he found the metal zipper. Outside, the sidewalk to the parking lot was shoveled. The car was caked in snow.

Plunging a bare hand through the powder and grasping the car handle, he broke it away from its icy constraints with a satisfying pop. A small avalanche came rushing down. The car warmed by the time he finished clearing snow off the front and back windshields, roof, and all four doors. He drove away from the firm with a sensation he had never felt before, but he wondered if this would give way to an avalanche of a different sort.

Sue was reading on the couch when he got to the apartment. She bookmarked her page and said, "Well, I'm dying to know how this went."

"It'll be a good client, but they have plans that I want to talk to you about."

"What are they doing?"

"This can't be shared with anyone, so keep it between us."

"What do they want you to do?"

"Negotiate a sale of goods and form a couple entities for them. They want to use the proceeds of the sale to fund American fighters in Ukraine, using the entities that I'll create for them."

"You're serious? Is that legal?"

"There's a way it could work. Americans can be paid once they are in Ukraine and have joined the Ukrainian forces. The issue would be recruiting and paying them in the United States. They aren't asking me to help with the recruitment specifics, though, just negotiate the sale and set up the entities. I would still advise on how to avoid violating the law since I know what they're planning."

"That still seems risky. I don't like that you'd be involved, even if you're just giving advice on the recruiting. What does the firm think? You're going to talk with them before taking it on, right?"

"I'm going to tell them exactly what I'm being hired for, which is legal services for the sale and the forming of business entities. This is an opportunity to make an impact, Sue. There is a real war going on, and it has the potential to destroy Ukraine and spread across Europe unless people do something about it. Everyone is hoping that Ukraine can hold off Putin's army, but they need support. We are on the right side of this."

Sue's chin rested in her hand as she gazed across the living room. Michael sat in a kitchen chair that he turned to face her. The main lamp was at a glow, the rest of the apartment dark. For a moment, he wished it was the set of a play, the stage furniture as fake as the problems. Sue was acting brilliantly as she did in school. She wasn't saying a word now, but she seemed to weigh the interests at stake with each breath, measuring love, fairness, compassion, and, perhaps most of all, trust. The gravity was in her eyes, in her stillness. Perhaps they could look out at the crowd at any moment and see the faces of families and children whispering too loud to their mothers for purse snacks or whatever they had that could be better than the show.

Would that be best? Michael thought. *To have all this be pretend? Has this all just been me amusing myself?* He knew it wasn't, and he knew that he had never been so clear-headed and willing.

"You barely know these people," Sue said.

"I feel like I know them more now."

"Yes, me, too," Sue said, scoffing.

"I liked Alexei. And despite everything, I do like Nikolai. I trust him."

"I suppose Kristelena knows about all of this?" Sue asked.

"I think she does."

"Why didn't they tell us about all of this before or be more up front?"

"I think they were trying to get to know us more, and Nikolai said I probably wouldn't have agreed to come to the meeting today if I knew the background, which is probably right."

"There are other ways to support Ukraine. You don't have to help out people who carry guns and want to secretly fund soldiers. There are militaries and governments for that sort of thing—leave it to them."

"Yes, but it's complicated. They need soldiers. They're not getting the help they need. There are people in the United States who would be willing to go fight, and I think it's unfair to ask only Ukrainians to fight and die in this war when the rest of the world has a stake in it."

"Could you lose your attorney license over this?"

"Not if it goes the way I think it can. There's always an option to withdraw myself if things start to go south."

"I understand the reasoning behind doing this, but you need to be very careful. If things aren't feeling right, you need to walk away. We need to walk away."

"I'll know more after getting the details from Alexei tomorrow," Michael said, then went to Sue and held her hand. "I'll know when to walk away if it comes to it."

Sue looked to Michael and then gazed at the other side of the room, her eyes catching the vibrant Marc Chagall print on the wall. As if added as a condition, she said, "I'm going to keep hanging out with Kristelena, and if I don't like how it's going, we're done with them."

8

"In person is better. Emails, text messages…they get leaked. It's not a matter of *if*, it's a matter of *when*," Alexei said. "I do have some papers for you. Now that you're our man, I will hand them off to you so that you can do your homework."

Michael held the phone firm against his ear. "That's fine with me."

"Make notes as you need, but only to the extent strictly necessary. No copies. Let's keep the paper trail on this tight, shall we?"

"Sure. Would you like to come to the firm to discuss?"

"I'd rather not come to that sad little asylum. Let's break you out of there instead."

Alexei asked if they could meet at a coffee shop. It was one of the large chains with the calorie content displayed next to each item.

At 10:30 a.m., Michael looked through the large glass windows of a scarcely populated coffee shop. Inside, Alexei's satchel and tan mackintosh were folded at an empty table in the corner. He must not have arrived long before. Steam billowed from his coffee cup as he leaned against the shop counter, flat cap pressed against his chest. The barista seemed to pour her soul out to him, gesturing with her hands. Alexei's head tilted towards her, demonstrating his concern.

It was odd to see a man with so much character inside a place with such a lack of it. It oscillated between upsetting and inspiring. The minimalistic, sleek interior, so uniform across all the chain's shops, clashed with Alexei's worldly persona and eclectic, well-worn clothes, which looked European but may not have been from the same country or even decade. His leather shoes looked English and possibly custom-made. He had donned a light grey turtleneck under a charcoal, plaid sport jacket that looked as much a part of him as his hair or arms. Then there was the familiar scent of black tea, mint, wet cobblestones.

"Ah, Michaael, good morning." Alexei took a second cup of coffee from the barista with a nod and handed it to Michael. "Let's get started, yes?" Alexei said. Warmly, he placed a hand on Michael's back and guided him toward the table. Somehow, like Collete's, this coffee shop had also transformed into Alexei's domain. The ability to make yourself comfortable in any setting is valuable, but Michael knew that the ability to make others feel comfortable in any setting was a high-level skill. People like Alexei won over the hearts and minds of others without them even realizing it. He was magnetic. "In this folder," Alexei began, taking the folder out from his satchel, "we have more details of the sale that we will finish together." He opened the folder and faced it toward Michael, spreading the papers so that each could be viewed. "You've probably seen all of this before...with maybe different details."

"Did the customer, Produktion Group AB Stockhom, provide a contract with terms they would want to use for the sale?"

"Yes," Alexei said, as he pulled a document from the back of the file and set it aside. "Before we...get in the weeds, let me give you a check for your retainer." From the breast pocket of his plaid jacket, Alexei withdrew and unfolded a check for $50,000 made out to Brower & Wood LLP. It was a personal check.

"Thank you, this will go in the trust account for your file, and we'll withdraw funds from it as I bill for my time," Michael said, acting on an assumption that Alexei did not have prior experience with this type of arrangement. But had he? Blood rushed to Michael's cheeks. "Thanks for the coffee as well. It's decent, but the main thing is I know from the board over there that it's two hundred calories. Don't expect me to deduct this from the retainer either, Alexei, it isn't that good."

"Ha ha. I wouldn't expect a lawyer to do such a thing. This simply proves you will be a strong negotiator for us." He placed the flat cap on the table and folded his hands together.

"Of course, but not so strong that I kill your deal."

"Exactly, and I should say," Alexei began and raised a finger, "we are willing to take on risk in this case because the sale is of great importance. If we can agree to something, we should. We are more wanting to decide points on...practical items, such as shipping and delivery terms and so forth, and the big, big items. To start with, there is our quotation for sale. You can see we offer fifty units for $10 million, so $200,000 each. The real cost for us to make these is about $25,000 each, but we have expertise, and we classify these as custom goods. Customers are willing to pay a good price for our expertise."

"So the Swedes are essentially paying far over the cost of the valves because they are specialized products?"

"Correct."

"That's a good profit margin."

"That's why I buy the company!" Alexei said with another hearty laugh.

"Do you make that margin on other sales?"

"No, this is a special sale. Now, here are the buyer's terms of purchase." Alexei passed a set of stapled documents across the table. The first page was cluttered with contractual provisions in small print.

"I can take these back to the office for review. We should negotiate some specific terms, such as shipping and payment, but this shouldn't be too bad if you're willing to take on a decent amount of risk. Do you have any more specific concerns?"

"You'll have plenty of time to review and discuss with me on our way," Alexei said, as if pointing out the obvious. He sipped from his coffee, watching Michael from the brim of the cup.

"On our way to where?"

"To Stockholm, of course."

"Sweden? For this deal?"

"Yes, this is the biggest deal we have ever had, Michael, and you know I prefer to do business in person. There is also potential to secure further business with this trip."

"When do you plan to go?"

"*We* are going tonight. You, me, and Oleg. This should not be a problem, no? I have paid your firm a large retainer; they should not have any reservations. Here are the flight details," Alexei said, handing Michael a folded piece of paper with a Delta flight number and departure time. "You can expense it on my bill."

"You can't be serious. Tonight? You expect me to fly to Stockholm tonight with less than a day's notice?"

"Why not? Do you have other matters at work? Anything going on with your wife? This is important, Michael. Everything rides on this," Alexei said, placing his hands together in plea with a soft smile.

"The flight is at 8:00 p.m. tonight?"

"Yes. Do you need a car to take you to the airport?"

"I should be able to arrange something with my wife. How long are we going for?"

"As long as it takes...I joke...we plan to come back in just one week, but you can purchase a ticket to return home if the negotiation is finished before then. Oleg and I have other business appointments so must stay longer." Alexei took a pull of his coffee and added, "maybe you will even have a nice time, who knows."

"Let me know wherever you need me," Michael said, regretting it as soon as he said it. "I wanted to tell you about some research as well. It's related to recruitment and distributing funds. I know you haven't engaged me for these questions, but I wanted to let you know that it appears to be illegal for you to pay or recruit volunteers within the United States for the purposes of sending them to Ukraine to fight. Officially, the United States is not at war with Russia, so this would breach US laws related to neutrality. However, if you are set on doing this, I'd advise that it does not appear illegal to recruit and pay American volunteers outside of the United States, which possibly includes recruitment through passive online channels, and recruitment outside the United States already happens with Americans signing up with the Ukrainian Foreign Legion. These volunteers are paid like other Ukrainian soldiers. I think you mentioned this example when we previously met."

"Bravo, Michael. Exactly. I have been in discussions with my people for months about this. You are correct that, essentially... organizing...this effort in the United States could create issues. This is why I mention that volunteers may sign up at the Ukrainian Embassy in the United States or online but that the volunteers do not get paid until they arrive in Ukraine. We are partnering with a non-governmental organization with operations abroad, in Ukraine, in order to fulfill our mission. It is a charity. They have... close ties to the Armed Forces of Ukraine and are active in helping one of the top brigades. Of course, it will make more impact if they have more money. They understand what we are trying to accomplish and will use the money specifically for this purpose."

Michael sat back in his chair and studied his hands. "And what purpose would this be, specifically?"

"Well, you are aware of the effort to provide funding for western troops. Remember I told you about all the bullshit around sending money to Ukraine? Not all donations are worthwhile. Like many other organizations and militaries, there are factions in the Ukrainian government and military. Sometimes aid does not even make it down to the military, and when it does, there are competing brigades. These brigades compete for resources, recruits, and standing within the military. These brigades are not all equal, so supporting one versus another is in…general sense important…as well as for short term goals. They all have specific aims they want to achieve within the broader war, targets that they want to hit. So, in this case, of course, we have a preference for what brigade we want to support with recruits and funds. For your purposes, assume all recruitment practices and distribution of funds to volunteers will ultimately and technically take place abroad."

"I'm curious. Do you personally know anyone in this specific brigade?"

"Yes, I know their leadership."

"And any distributions of funds you make will be to the non-governmental organization you mentioned?"

"That is correct."

"That would be better for you than funding the volunteers through your newly created businesses. Will you still want the new business entities and bank accounts organized so that you can withdraw funds from Minnesota Instruments, LLC?" Michael asked, then glanced at his watch. It was 10:50 a.m.

Alexei gave a knowing nod and added, "We still need the additional business entities and bank accounts organized so that we may transfer funds from those accounts. That reminds me, here are our banking details." Alexei withdrew a folder from his satchel and handed it to Michael. "I believe you will need to contact our bank to arrange payment with the Swedish buyer. You can also establish bank accounts for the new entities with this bank."

Michael studied the contents of the folder, recognized the name of the same national bank that was on Alexei's personal check, and verified that the account was a business account for Minnesota Instruments, LLC. "When you make the payments from the new business accounts to the non-governmental organization, I would make it a transfer outside of the US. It sounds like the non-governmental organization, the charity, is located abroad."

"Your point is taken, Michael, thank you. I will discuss this with Oleg, but I believe this is the plan. The charity is located abroad. Its main operation is in Ukraine."

"Can I ask what the charity is called?"

"Free East, and the brigade is called Blue Scepter. With these names especially, Michael, let's not send these through email or text message. Don't even do a TikTok song about this."

Michael laughed and replied, "I won't, I promise. I will reach out to your bank to ask for a draft letter of credit for the transaction. They should be able to provide this within a day or two so that we can present it to the Swedish buyer. The buyer will want to give our draft to their bank, which is called the issuing bank in this situation, and that bank will confirm our letter of credit is acceptable or maybe add a few modifications. The bottom line is payment for the goods will ultimately come from the buyer's bank."

"I'm not sure the buyer will allow you to speak with their bank; they are very protective of their operations."

"I don't need to speak with their bank. They can make that request themselves. I'm sure their contract asks for some type of confidentiality on the sale as well."

"Well, Michael," Alexei said as he started gathering papers together, "you will take these documents with you, pack your bags, and give my apologies to your wife for stealing you away on short notice. I will see you at the airport. We plan to meet at the diner near our gate one hour before the flight. Join us."

In the car, Michael called Katherine with the flight details and asked that she book a ticket as soon as possible, no return trip necessary for now. "And also," Michael added, "I got a large retainer from Alexei, do you think the partners will be upset if I leave the country for a few days? I feel obligated because that's where the buyer is located and Alexei is set on it. He's one of those guys that prefers to do business in person."

"You better hope that check clears," Katherine replied with a muffled laugh. "Do you need my assistance over there? I think it will be fine. Are you going to come back to the office and give them a heads up? Not sure if you want to leave that as a message for me to give them."

"Yes, I'm heading there after lunch. Thanks. I'll bring you back some Swedish meatballs from the trip, but I think that's the best I can do. How's that sound?

"Just peachy. See you soon."

Michael hung up the phone and paused before putting the car in drive. *Why didn't Alexei tell me he was aware of the recruiting issue in the United States?* he thought. *Maybe they truly don't need my help with that aspect of the plan, which is more than fine with me. Maybe they know I wouldn't take this on if that was part of the representation. Can I expense a first-class ticket? That would eat up the retainer. Don't get distracted, keep your eye on the ball. One step at a time. Withdraw if you need to, even if that means leaving Sweden early.*

As he drove away from the coffee shop, Michael imagined sitting in a room with the Swedish buyer and two possible scenarios: (a) the buyer has no idea they are paying far over what they need to for the goods and are unaware of what Alexei ultimately plans to do with his profits, or (b) a possibly worse situation, the buyer knows exactly what the plan is and desires to fund troops, no, fund a specific brigade, in Ukraine as part of the deal. The buyer will be extremely polite regardless of the circumstances. Swedes are difficult to read.

There were nine hours before departure. Michael phoned Nikolai and asked to meet for lunch. He bought two cold sandwiches from a drive thru and drove to the parking lot of Nikolai's dental office. Nikolai appeared outside in his parka and walked swiftly through the cold to Michael's car in his Nike tennis shoes. "It's colder than...a well digger's ass outside," Nikolai said. "That's how it goes, right?"

"That's cute," Michael said, handing Nikolai a sandwich.

"I just had coffee with Alexei. He wants me to go to Sweden with him tonight."

"Lucky you. I'd go, but I don't know if I'd be able to get back into the country."

"You better stay back. The team would be destroyed if you got denied at the border. Not sure if you're invited anyway. Listen, you said before that you're not sure how much the buyer knows about the transaction...do you know anything new about them?"

"Not really, I can tell you that they are legitimately buying goods."

"Does the buyer know that they are over-paying for the goods?"

"I think so...do you really want to know?"

"Tell me whatever you know."

"I can't tell you everything I know."

"Tell me what you can. I'm not going to do this dance every time with you."

"Don't write this down anywhere," he said as he glanced over his shoulder and lowered his voice. "I can't say for sure, but I think the Swedish buyer has some government behind them...a Swedish intelligence agency. The buyer is aligned with them or is part of them. I'm not sure."

"Why would they do that? Isn't Sweden already providing military aide like the US and everyone else?"

"Politics, and, like Alexei said, bullshit. The whole point is that Alexei and the others want control over these funds. The military aide going through the formal channels gets lost, there's no control. From my understanding, the Swedish intelligence community is getting pressure on one side of their government to be way too conservative, just shove money at Ukraine and call it job done. Put it in the bucket with money from the rest of the countries, as long as the Ukrainian flag is on it. Another part of the government wants to be more aggressive. My understanding is that the Swedes must try very hard to do anything...officially...beyond simple economic or humanitarian support because some in the government do not want to offer much for military aide. There is a specific...effort... that Alexei and the Swedish buyer want to support. To do this, they need more control than the formal channels will allow. Many Swedish politicians would not be pleased with going outside the formal channels, favoring a specific Ukrainian brigade, or directly supporting the recruitment of *American* volunteers."

"And they know that it's illegal to do the recruitment and funding in the US, right?"

"Not sure, but practically, it will be abroad. Maybe just online, who knows," Nikolai said as he ripped into the sandwich, salami dangling from its edge. "Do you have any mustard? I love mustard."

"It's in the bag. Why doesn't Alexei just work with the Swedes and do this whole thing abroad, including raising the funds?"

"Because Alexei's business is in the US. The sale covers up the transfer of funds to Alexei, and Alexei can put the funds in the right place. He is the connection. For political reasons, like I said, the Swedish buyer doesn't want to make it obvious that they are organizing this type of effort."

This "effort." What a fittingly vague word for this whole arrangement. "Why don't they just do this with the American military or American intelligence services? The US and Sweden are on the same side."

"Ha. Again, politics. The Americans and Swedes don't have the same objectives or...skin in the game. The Americans also don't have the time of day for Sweden. If they want to do this within the time it should be done, they need to act now. Most importantly, they want to recruit American volunteers with military experience. The United States would never participate in this type of recruitment. They have their own operatives and agenda. Maybe they are using all of the Ukrainian army for their own agenda. It's a bigger chess board for them. The whole thing might be blown if the United States' intelligence services even knew about it. They probably prefer not to know so that they don't have to try and stop us. Like you said, we're on the same side."

"What is the non-governmental organization that Alexei is talking about? Free East?"

"I help out Free East sometimes, unofficially. Then again, every-thing Free East does is unofficial, except for...what they officially do to be a charity...and they actually do a good amount of that to be fair."

"What do you do for Free East? Hang up posters at the mall?" Michael jabbed, hoping to God it wasn't bank robbery or assassi-nations.

"Sometimes I make introductions for them, mainly with people from Eastern Europe who have settled here."

"Is that how you met Alexei?"

"No, Alexei is way above my...pay grade...yes? We met another way, through mutual friends."

"Does Kristelena work for Free East?"

"Take a breath, Michael. Slow down. Did I scare you off with the information about the Swedish buyer? It should make you feel better if they know they aren't being taken advantage of."

"No, I'm not walking away yet, but I still haven't told my firm or Sue that I'm leaving the country tonight."

"Bring Sue, she'll love it. Go, and think of me flossing teeth in the Midwest while you enjoy your fancy European dinners," Nikolai said as he wrapped up the rest of his sandwich and stuffed it into the pocket of his parka.

"You know I appreciate all the information you can give me."

"*Pozhaluysta*, my friend."

9

"Do you know where Sondheim is?" Michael asked when he approached Katherine's desk.

"Let me check his calendar. It looks like he's in, and you could catch him before his three o'clock."

"Thanks, here's the retainer check. Fingers crossed. I'll be over the Atlantic by the time it gets cleared or rejected. Do you think I should let anyone else know I'm leaving or just Sondheim? He's senior and the nicest, so seems like the path of least resistance."

"I'd ask Sondheim and tell anyone else you're working with after Sondheim approves."

"Brilliant, thanks. I'll check back in before I leave. I'll be heading out shortly to pack and then get on the road. By the way, let's just do a physical file for this one. Alexei doesn't like email, so everything will be done either live or on hard copy."

"I'll put a physical file together—want me to make copies of those?" Katherine asked, pointing to the file Michael had under his arm.

"No, that's okay. Thanks." He gripped it under his arm, making it curl.

Michael did not tip toe around corners now. He walked with

purpose and resolve. The confidence in his approach mattered. If he asked Sondheim about the trip with too much deference, Sondheim would shoot him down and advise him to tell Alexei that the matter can be supported remotely from Minnesota, that there were ongoing matters at the firm that also need attention, and that it was too short notice. His communication to Sondheim had to be framed as if the whole matter was hinging on Michael's ability to travel to Sweden for the negotiation, which probably was the truth, though Michael did not put up too much of a fight.

"Remember when we talked about me getting my own book of business together?" he asked Sondheim. He shut the door behind him and took a seat in front of Sondheim's desk. *Should I sit back and put my feet up on his desk?* Michael thought to himself in amusement.

"Yes, how are things going? You know, there are lots of local events and professional groups in the area that you could join to try and attract clients. That's how I got a lot of clients early in my career."

"I'll definitely keep that in mind. Actually, something recently came about organically out of a friend on my hockey team. Have you ever heard of Minnesota Instruments, LLC?"

"Good for you, but no, I've never heard of that company."

"The client is Alexei Stakhanovich, and he's the sole owner of the company. They make safety valves for factories and things like that. Alexei recently bought all the shares of this company, and he just secured a major buyer in Sweden. I agreed to represent him in the negotiation and help out with some other things, like entity organization. He just gave us a $50,000 retainer fee as well—I didn't ask him for it, but he preferred to do it that way so he could make sure he's a priority."

"That's excellent. Look at you. Rain maker, eh? You like contracts and business matters, too, don't you?"

"This is exactly the type of practice I'd like to build out. Also, though, I wanted to talk to you because I met with Alexei today and he wants me to fly to Sweden with him *tonight* in order to do the negotiation in person over the next few days. I already took him on as a client, and I think this is kind of a deal-breaker for him. Lucky for me, I guess. I wanted to give you a heads up and see if there would be any big issues with me leaving the country for a few days."

"Lucky you, indeed. Still, tell him no. We need you here."

"He won't go for that, John."

"Tell him I made you stay."

"No, I can't do that. He'll go with someone else."

"Fine. If he's a client, has given that retainer, and that's what he needs you to do, you'd better go. It'll probably be easier to conduct the negotiation in person anyway. You could ask Dalton to step in on any research assignments or things like that. Maybe even Macomber."

"No, it's good timing, there's nothing that pressing or that I can't keep up on from Sweden. We're waiting on a reply for Macomber. Sounds good, John. I'll send a note to everyone I'm working with to let them know, and I'll send you a post card."

Walking the hall back from Sondheim's office, Michael debated turning around and telling the whole story. His chest felt heavy. *But then what?* he thought to himself, *call the whole thing off? Things are never black and white. If you want to do something of real consequence, you have to be willing to put yourself on the line. Take the damn risk for the greater purpose.*

"Katherine, it's done. Operation Swedish meatball is a go," Michael said as he walked by Katherine's desk and started gathering things in his office. Not one for raising her voice, Katherine walked to Michael's doorway.

"He was for it, then?"

"Eventually."

"When will you be back? I'll block your calendar off."

"You can just block it off for the next week. Thanks."

"Sure, and can you call me with your passport information

when you get home? I'll need that to book your ticket. Looks like there's plenty of seats on the flight still. I guess Sweden isn't a major destination in January."

"Right, I'll call you when I get home." Michael walked with purpose again through the halls, around corners, and finally through the steel staff door and into the chilled air. The air burned his lungs, but he was alive and clear headed. He watched his breath leave him and dissipate into the grey sky, meditating on it briefly as he stood just outside the door, feeling the ice and pavement salt beneath his boots.

Sue would be getting home from work in an hour. He tore out of the parking lot, burst through a snow barrier left by the city plow, and sped home.

On arrival, Michael pulled his passport out of his desk drawer and phoned Katherine. "There are still tickets left for the 8 p.m. flight. Do you want a window seat?" she asked.

"That will work," Michael said as he walked to the kitchen and prepared a pot of coffee.

"Great, you'll be getting the email confirmation. Safe trip!"

"Thanks, Katherine," Michael said, hanging up the phone and then adding water to the back of the coffee machine. He studied the flight details once again. The first plane would depart from Minneapolis and arrive in Amsterdam mid-morning. After a three-hour layover, the next plane would take them to Stockholm. He packed quickly and then changed into one of the three sport jackets he would have in Stockholm. After bringing a bag into the entry way, Michael paused, then decided to take it back to the bedroom so as not to overwhelm Sue with a packed bag near the front door. With time to spare, he poured a cup of coffee and opened the file he obtained from Alexei. His hands were somehow still cold despite the running around. It could have been the nerves. He placed the quotation of sale in front of him. Before reading it, he wrapped his hands around the coffee cup, wishing it was a crystal ball. *Tell me how this ends,* he whispered to himself as he stared into the black coffee and examined the oils.

The quotation was concise and as Alexei described. There were fifty industrial valves offered for ten million US Dollars, subject to Minnesota Instrument, LLC's standard terms and conditions located on its website at the link provided. Even accounting for other costs and expenses, the sale should generate a substantial profit if the cost of the valves was $25,000 each. Michael replayed Alexei's explanation in his head, "Customers are willing to pay a good price for our expertise," especially if that expertise is covertly supporting a Ukrainian military brigade. Pushing the quotation aside, he extracted the buyer's terms and conditions from the file and scanned the provisions.

All these legal provisions—what did it even matter if this wasn't the transaction the parties actually cared about? What was Alexei worried about? Maybe, as is often the case, Alexei just wanted a lawyer to spot potential issues for him. Michael sipped his coffee and thought as he peered out the window at snow covered branches. *Alexei mentioned payment...he wants to make sure he gets paid, and, similarly, he would want to make sure he doesn't have to give the money back.* Even if the valves weren't the real focus of this transaction, the money would still be tied to the contract and Alexei could either benefit or suffer from its terms. It will still be an enforceable contract despite the secrecy in the background. Everything within the four corners of the documents appeared to consider a sale of goods, nothing more.

Turning the pages over and scanning paragraphs, Michael located the Payment Terms section and was drawn to one item that stood out. In size ten font, Michael read: "Payment shall be due net forty-five days from Buyer's receipt of invoice and goods, provided such invoice and goods are deemed satisfactory to Buyer, in Buyer's sole discretion." The clause could give the buyer a basis for delaying payment far beyond forty-five days after the original invoice was sent.

He stopped. The sound of footsteps neared the door. *Would Sue want to go with him on the trip?* He should have looked into it, but it was probably too short notice for her to get off work. Michael gathered the transaction documents in a neat pile on the table, as was his habit after reading anything, and approached the door to greet her with his metaphoric hat in hand.

He was surprised when he heard a solid knock before he got to the door. Looking through the peephole, he saw Oleg standing on the doormat with his hands tucked in the pockets of his grey peacoat, intense eyes staring down the steps from the doorway. His hat did not appear in hand. *Is this guy going to push me down the stairs if I open up?* Michael thought. He opened the door, resisting the urge to keep it cracked.

"I just want to make sure you are up for this," Oleg said. "Alexei has a tendency to get excited and other people don't want to let him down by saying no. Are you ready for this?"

"Definitely, won't be a problem. I'm excited to be joining you."

"Excellent, and don't worry about so much of the details...as long as you cover anything that would be a major concern."

"Understood."

"We all have a role here. You won't even have access to the funds in the accounts, or you shouldn't. If the bank asks you about this— asks about any account details—or has questions about processing, just let me know. With the new accounts, just set them up at the bank and request that me and Alexei have access. Got it?"

"That's no problem, I usually don't do any actual money management for clients," Michael said, feeling fortunate that he would not be privy to whatever financial maneuvering was to transpire.

"Have you called the bank yet about the letter of credit for the buyer's payment?"

"No, but I can before I leave. I just got packed."

"Good, Michael, no problem," Oleg said, nodding and inspecting Michael's apartment over his shoulder.

"Why haven't you bought a house? This isn't New York City you know, you should be able to afford one."

"We've been saving up to buy something."

"Look, you are busy. I will let you go." Oleg turned and walked down the steps. After saying goodbye, Michael waited in vain for a reply. He shut the door after Oleg's footsteps faded.

Sue was running late. He pulled out Alexei's banking details and searched online for the bank's letter of credit services. On its website, Michael located the phone number listed for letter of credit requests and connected with a bank representative.

He informed them that his client needed a letter of credit to secure an international transaction and provided Minnesota Instruments, LLC's account information as well as his contact information as the owner's counsel. On the other end of the line, the representative typed quickly and advised that he could provide the bank's standard letter of credit template if Michael was able to fill in the details of the transaction, such as total price, delivery date, and the buyer's entity information. "I can send it to your email address," he added, over the sound of his tapping.

Give me the letter template that your bank uses to secure payment from a foreign intelligence agency, Michael thought to himself over the continued tapping, *on the off chance that my client gets stuck with a bill for a military unit in Ukraine, I'd like my client to ensure he's able to collect the money from the foreign intelligence operatives in play and deposit that money in his account with your esteemed institution...I'm sure you've got one of those letters sitting around...check under miscellaneous.*

"The bank's standard letter of credit will be fine, thanks," Michael said.

"Sure thing, on its way now. Any correspondence can be sent to the email address associated with forthcoming email. May I help you with anything else today, sir?"

"No, thank you," Michael responded as he watched Sue's car

pull carefully into the garage outside the window. A pit formed in his stomach. "I shouldn't need anything else."

10

"Do you have your passport, cell phone, computer?" Sue asked, turning her blinker off as she merged onto the highway.

Michael nodded then peered out the window. "Thanks again for the ride. And for understanding."

"Sure, I mean, it'll hopefully be a nice experience, and what else would you do? Drop him as a client? Just promise you'll be careful," Sue added, looking to Michael, then to the road, and back to Michael with her caring eyes. Both her hands gripped the wheel as they forged through light swirls of snow dancing unpredictably on the road.

"I promise," Michael said, taking her right hand and holding it in both of his, leaving Sue's left hand steady on the wheel. The small diamond on her engagement ring sparkled in the grey winter light like a mystical beacon, perhaps guiding or warning them.

Sue put the car in park at the airport departures door. She turned to Michael, more pale than usual. "I love you. Safe travels, okay?"

Michael stroked her cheek. "I love you, too. I will let you know when I land." They kissed inside the car before unloading Michael's bag from the trunk.

The airport was desolate. Alexei and Oleg were not in sight. Michael checked in his luggage, obtained a paper boarding pass, and proceeded through the security line swiftly. The flight gate was on the far end of the terminal. Sweat began to form on his upper lip as he walked the polished halls.

The information display indicated the flight to Amsterdam was on time. As Michael neared his gate, a diner appeared in the corner with a good view of the tarmac. Alexei and Oleg sat at a corner table eating omelets and rye toast. They drank light beer.

"Michael, excellent. Please join us," Alexei said, standing to greet Michael and pulling out a chair.

"Looks like the flight is on time, you never know what can happen with these winter flights from MSP," Michael said.

"Right, it will be okay, I think. You see our plane there now." Alexei pointed out the window at the Airbus. Carts and airport personnel swarmed around it like worker bees around a hive, preparing the plane for what Michael hoped was not the beginning of an odyssey.

"You will eat here Michael or wait for airplane food?" Alexei asked.

"We have some time. I'll have the same as you two. Breakfast for dinner is fine since there are no rules in an airport."

"I like it. I think he will be easy to travel with," Alexei said as he turned to Oleg, who scooped egg onto his toast with precision. He sprinkled salt into his hand, felt it between his bony fingers, then delicately applied some of it to his egg before discarding the remainder on the midnight black tiles beneath the table.

A group of four men in their twenties unloaded their luggage at a nearby table and said something about bloody mary's. Michael guessed they were a touring band based on their sticker-covered equipment cases. The waiter appeared in the dining room suddenly, as if from a trap door. He noticed the new arrivals and gracefully leaned to pick up a stack of menus from the front counter as he made his way. It could have been twenty new patrons or one, his demeanor said it was all the same. Up close, the waiter was older and more good-humored than Michael expected. He had tan skin, grey stubble, and wore a white dress shirt tucked into navy chinos. His sleeves were rolled up carefully like a barber's.

"Fellas," he interjected quietly and with good timing, placing a menu in front of Michael.

"I'll just have what they're having, thanks."

"You sure? The burgers are good here. Goes better with beer as well."

"That sounds better," Michael said, mostly wanting to satisfy the waiter by taking his suggestion.

The waiter turned to the group of young men, "well, here's trouble I can tell..."

Alexei winced. "I should have got the burger, I will miss the burger on our trip. Michael, I suppose you can study some materials on the flight. You will have a chance to do this in Stockholm as well. We will not meet with the buyer until the day after we arrive."

"That will be better with the jet leg. I will do more preparing ahead of the meeting, but I wanted to tell you about a potential issue in the buyer's terms and get your impression." Michael pulled out the file with the transaction documents. "See, I was looking at the payment terms section...are you worried about not getting paid?"

Alexei placed his napkin on his plate and pushed it aside. "There are many stakeholders in the background. We trust our contacts, but some things might be out of their control, so we have to prepare for the possibility of the buyer trying to back out."

Michael sat with the file sitting unopened in front of him. "You should know," he began after a subtle scan of the dining area, "Nikolai told me about the connection with the Swedish buyer. It sounds like they ultimately want the same thing as you, so why do you have concerns?"

Alexei folded his hands together and raised his thumbs, a sliver of a grin on his face. "We would have told you eventually about the buyer having a...similar agenda. Sorry, Michael." Alexei scanned the dining area now but continued in a perfectly inconspicuous tone. "Had you decided not to join us on this trip, it would have been unnecessary for you to know this information. To address your question, and as I said before, it could potentially be an issue with the buyer refusing to pay even if we have trusted contacts on their side. It's not that we will pay out funds before we receive payment for the goods, but we will be making promises before we receive the money from the buyer. Nikolai told you that the buyer has a connection with...the Swedish government, I believe, yes?"

"In a way, yes."

"It is true, but the buyer is not totally government. There is something like a partnership between a man whose family has a large ownership interest in Produktion Group AB Stockholm and the government contacts. His name is Mattias von Andersson."

Michael glanced down and blinked hard. It had been over a year since he had heard the name. He raised his head after a moment and met Alexei's eyes.

"He will be in Stockholm," Alexei said, holding Michael's gaze. "He is an executive of the company and has power in the organization." With a hand flourish, Alexei leaned back and added, "However, there are other people in the company, and perhaps in government, that might not look...kindly...on this arrangement. Therefore, yes, we have worry about Mattias being able to see this through. He assures us that it will happen."

Michael turned to Oleg, who was sitting with his arms folded in front of him, then glanced back at Alexei. *What do they know? What do I know? Play it through,* Michael thought. "I'd advise that it's worth fixing the issues I picked up with the payment terms. It could otherwise allow the buyer to delay payment indefinitely. For example, if there was disagreement at Produktion Group AB Stockholm or pressure from the government that led to uncertainty about going through with the sale."

Michael opened the file and drew attention to the clauses at issue. "In my opinion," Michael said, "this could give the buyer too much control over when to submit payment, mainly because the payment obligation is only triggered after the buyer decides the invoice and the goods are acceptable. Of course, if you actually provide the goods, there's not much of an argument to be made that the buyer does not owe you anything. Rather, it could cost you valuable time in getting paid."

The waiter arrived and set a burger and beer to Michael's side, away from the papers. "Anything else for you all?" he asked, clasping his hands together as waiters do when there is nothing left for them to offer. Alexei requested the check for all three meals and gave his compliments for the service. The group of young men reacted loudly to something in their conversation and clanked their glasses together in a cheers.

"I wouldn't want you to make promises to other people and not be able to back it up," Michael said, looking to both Alexei and Oleg. "And I wouldn't want to be involved with a delay like that myself. I'm going to suggest some simple revisions in the negotiation to cover it."

"This is precisely why we needed a lawyer," Alexei said to Oleg. "This is the sort of question I want you to be asking yourself during the negotiation, Michael, things that could really matter for us, but don't make it obvious that we have worries about them trying to back out of the sale. I agree with your suggestions. I want there to be obligations, not loopholes. I believe Mattias does as well. We just have to...subtly put these intentions into the terms."

"Make sure the letter of credit information is included," Oleg said.

"Of course."

"Have you received a copy of the letter of credit from our bank?" Oleg asked.

"Yes, I have. I can print it out from my email at our hotel. I could also email it to the buyer now so that they have more time to ask their bank about it."

"Let's give it to them in person. They can email it to their bank themselves if that is necessary. I would like you to keep the negotiated items to a minimum if possible. Let's say...pick five of your biggest items and we will negotiate those. I would like this to move along quickly."

A ding sounded in the gate area followed by a boarding call for Amsterdam. The group of young men and the waiter made eye contact. The waiter went to the register and printed their bill. Alexei and Oleg slowly gathered their things.

"I'll stay back and finish. There will be some time until I need to board," Michael said.

"Have a nice flight. We'll see you in Amsterdam," Alexei said, as he tucked his scarf into his carry-on bag and pulled out a copy of *The Economist*, placing his boarding pass and passport between the pages. The waiter arrived with the check and Alexei withdrew several bills from a money clip that had a comical array of different currencies. Alexei must have felt Michael's eyes and noted, "Cash is king, as they say."

Passengers crowded at the entrance to the jet walk. Alexei and Oleg stood outside the diner but at a distance away from anyone. *For all the overlap between Minnesota and Canada*, Michael thought, *it was disappointing that Minnesotans didn't fully adopt the Canadian tendency to wait patiently to board until their zone was called.* Michael finished his last bites and stayed seated.

"You all in a band touring around?" Michael asked the group nearby. The question sounding more envious than he would have liked.

"Trying to be," one of them replied. He shrugged.

"Is Amsterdam your end destination?"

"No, we are going on to Berlin. My uncle owns a club there, so we will play a series of shows in Berlin for one month and then maybe travel somewhere else in Germany. Are you going on a work trip with those other guys?"

"Yeah, heading to Sweden with those two," Michael said, pointing to Alexei and Nikolai.

"You might want to give the third one a shout. He might miss the plane."

"It's just the three of us. Was someone else here?"

"We saw the serious one over there talking to someone in the coffee shop a few gates down before we came to eat. Looked like they were travelling together, but maybe not." The band hauled their cases towards the jet walk. Michael lingered behind.

11

Michael ran through the woods on a snow-covered path. The sodden snowflakes splashed his face, blurring his vision. He drove his knees up and plunged his feet to the ground, gaining speed. He could feel time running out and the gap getting smaller. As he exhaled, a blow to the right side of his rib cage dropped him to the ground. He looked up at the bush with snow covered eyelashes. A deer peered back with sharp blue eyes and continued into the woods.

There was a tap on his shoulder. He woke with a start.

"Would you like chicken or vegetarian?" he heard faintly.

"No, thank you," he managed to mumble.

The flight attendant lingered so he shook his head and said it once more. He switched on the reading light above his head and withdrew his glasses from the breast pocket of his Oxford shirt. He let his eyes re-gain focus, then pulled the transaction file and a small notebook and pen from the bag underneath the seat in front of him.

Alexei wants to limit to five things, he thought to himself. Reviewing the terms line by line under the small, overhead spotlight, he picked out language he normally would and saved it for future consideration. He listed these items in the notebook with a reference to the section number and a star-rating between zero and three based on severity. Any language that could allow the buyer to suspend, cancel, or seek immediate refund received the highest rating of severity. Things that had potential to create liability for Alexei's company in the long term were left on the list for Alexei's attention but not assigned a rating.

He set his pen down to rest and noticed there were barely any other reading lights on in the cabin. Feeling accomplished, exhausted, and guilty about his reading light, he placed the file, notebook, and pen back in the bag underneath the seat and switched the light off. He leaned against the cool window and shut his heavy eyes, though his heart still pounded.

In Amsterdam, they ate Dutch pancakes, which Alexei described as "sumptuous" with bagged eyes and genuine satisfaction. They inhaled coffee as Michael presented his findings on the buyer's legal terms and conditions. Alexei and Oleg nodded as he proceeded through his list, appreciating the simplification of issues and the rating system Michael employed.

"Mattias will be in the room with us to push the negotiation along as well," Alexei added. "He will be reasonable and try to speed things up. It will help if we just have a few requests to go over and otherwise accept their terms. Mattias has probably never read their legal terms and conditions, but I am sure he would appreciate closing any openings that would allow the company to avoid the sale."

"He needs to make sure his guys fall in line," Oleg said. He took a sip of coffee and pursed his lips.

The meal was reviving Alexei. "Mattias is a good man...an interesting man," he went on. "He comes from a very old Swedish family, one of the oldest noble families, actually. It doesn't mean much in Sweden these days, probably for good reason. The noble families have mostly been stripped of their privileges over the years, though I think some were able to keep timber farms in the far north."

Oleg laughed and said, "You think I give a shit? This is not Disney channel with princes."

Alexei shrugged and placed a hand on Oleg's shoulder. "I think *this* Disney prince did not get any rest on the plane. What do you think, Michael?"

"I think it's early or late, I'm not sure. Where are we staying in Stockholm?"

"Where else other than the Grand Hotel near the Royal Palace and Gamla Stan?"

"I've walked by it, but never stayed," Michael said.

"The Grand Hotel is exceptional," Oleg said, sucking in his breath and swirling his coffee. "But the last time I was there, I almost strangled a man in the sauna."

"I could not think of a worse death," Alexei said. He lost interest and turned to study passers-by.

"This fat Swede kept going on about the Coca-Cola acquisition of Costa Coffee, asking me to guess how much they paid for it. I swear I almost held his face to the goddamn coals," Oleg said, putting his hands together in a pushing down motion. He had meaty palms with short fingers and wore a gold, link bracelet on his wrist.

The plane for the flight to Stockholm was smaller than the one from Minneapolis to Amsterdam. The weather was calm, and it seemed the plane began its descent shortly after reaching its peak altitude. Stockholm's Arlanda airport was clean and frigid.

They took a black Mercedes taxi-van to the Grand Hotel and checked in with a cheery woman running the counter. Michael moved on to the business center before finding his room. He printed out five copies of the letter of credit template the bank sent to his email and read it twice. His room was on the fourth floor. It had blue walls and an off-white ceiling with crown molding. He set his things on the plush, red divan and drew back thick curtains in front of the window to reveal Saltsjön bay. The large brick and stone Royal Palace appeared across the waterway. Lights illuminated the palace walls from below. He called Sue while he stood in front of the window and hoped she would be on her lunch break. The phone rang twice.

"Well, what is it like there?" she asked after giving Michael updates from home.

"It's a long way from west Duluth," Michael said, peering around the curtain to look down the street.

"I miss you," she said.

"I miss you, too."

"Can you come back?"

"Sure, I'll grab a cab now. I won't even have to unpack."

"Or you could send me a ticket, and I could come lay down the law. I'd protect you."

"I know you would; they wouldn't want any of that smoke."

"Tell me more about it there and then let's talk about something else. You're in love with it, aren't you?"

"It's old. Stately. I can't imagine all the history this small piece of land has seen over the years. It's been through peace, war, and everything in between."

"You're somewhere between now."

12

Mattias von Andersson fidgeted with the silverware next to his plate. "But I've chosen this venue to illustrate the gravity of the situation," he said. The others looked on in anticipation. Mattias continued, "In 1938, the Nazi politician Franz von Papen was hosted for a dinner at this hotel, in this very dining room. As the story goes, Von Papen told the party that the next time he was in Sweden, he hoped to walk on German ground. Despite Sweden's neutrality, there were Nazi sympathizers at all levels of society, from sailors in the port at Gotland to high-ranking members of the government, many of whom were at that dinner in 1938."

Mattias paused, dabbing his upper lip with the fold of his napkin. "They say people in the dining room cheered. Can you imagine? Von Papen could have been sitting where you are now. *You* could have been sitting in the audience then. What would you have done? It was a complicated situation. Back then, Stockholm was not an obvious part of the war ground, but there were spies everywhere, and it was a very different sort of war." He turned a fork over on its prongs and balanced it by pressing his index finger to the other end, still holding the attention of the table.

"There were Nazi spies among us Swedes, of course, and some

not-so-secret promoters, but there was also a Swedish opposition to the Nazis. Swedish intelligence operatives worked to gather information and subvert German interests. One of these operatives was my grandfather, who worked alongside the famous English diplomat and spy known as Karlsson. My grandfather was an art historian. Recruited by C-byrån, or C-Bureau, to get close to the Nazis in Stockholm. He was at that dinner in 1938, and I'm here now, in a similarly difficult time for our country and for the free world as we know it. I am a Swedish patriot, and I'll be damned if the Russians get as close to us as the Nazis did. This is why I invite you here, to my country, to this hotel, to this room."

"Well said, Mattias. To Sverige," Alexei said, raising a linen-white coffee cup. The others joined.

Mattias wore a tweed suit complete with an English waist coat, burgundy polka dot tie, and crisp white pocket square. His watch was from A. Lange & Söhne: a classic Lange 1 with a navy-blue face and leather band. A collectible.

It was the only table of guests in the vast dining room. Michael estimated that Mattias reserved the entire space. It was ornate, with red carpet and chairs, gold trimmings on the walls, and an extravagant chandelier hanging from the middle of the ceiling which glistened in the morning sun.

"Further to Mattias' point," Alexei said, "I can't express my opinion enough of the...criticalness...of defending this first nation, my nation, that Putin has attempted to invade. Every nation of the West is watching. If this first line of defense falls, it will be viewed as a sign of weakness and...undoubtedly...the opportunity will be seized to...to drive a wedge into the West....to make countries feel isolated....to have doubts of even the NATO alliance and nations' true willingness to stand their ground. Momentum is, like in many aspects of life and politics, the driver of perceptions first, then of reality itself."

Two other Swedes accompanied Mattias at the table. There was a woman in her forties with blond hair pulled back in a bun and fashionable black glasses. She wore a white blouse, black business skirt, and black heels. Between her and Mattias was a tall, slim man in his late fifties with wire rimmed glasses. He wore a grey flannel suit and brown double monk strap shoes. They listened with attentiveness and deference, not appearing excited nor concerned. They were interested, focused, measured.

"However, enough of my grand talk. We still have not introduced everyone at this table," continued Alexei. "Some of you already know Oleg, my business associate, and this is Michael, our lawyer. Michael is young, but he has read old books as they say. We have come here with an open mind and a determination to find... common ground. Michael, you should know, studied law in Sweden at Uppsala University, but he is an American lawyer. We will pause now to welcome any jokes that you might have about the legal profession, but to be fair, know that all jokes will apply equally to lawyers of all countries. It is a universal...vileness."

"How do you *stand* this man?" Mattias jabbed. "But I know, he is one of those people who keeps things interesting...these are my associates. This is Alice, let's call her my personal business adviser. She does not work at the company but is advising on the deal we are making together. And this is Emil, who is also a lawyer. Emil studied at Uppsala University as well, Michael." Mattias identified both of them with an open-faced hand. His grin at Michael lingered.

An assortment of dishes was brought to the table, including cardamom buns, fresh fruit, hard boiled eggs with caviar, and bagels topped with salmon, dill, and capers. Michael was starved and he resisted the urge to eat quickly. He tore a warm cardamom bun apart—its bready aroma seemed to fill the cracks in his stomach.

"Uppsala," began Emil, "is known as having the least vile law school in Europe."

"I may have missed this, Emil, but are you a lawyer for Produktion Group AB Stockholm or Mattias?" Michael asked, as Emil continued to raise his coffee cup to his freshly shaven face. Silverware clanked around the table as Emil considered his response for a moment. He set his cup down on the saucer in front of him.

"Forgive me, I'm sure you know us Swedes are mad about coffee." He cleared his throat and adjusted his glasses. "Strictly speaking, I am acting as neither Mattias' nor Production Group's lawyer. I am playing more of a business role, using my legal background. I am not wearing the lawyer's hat. I focus on strategic partnerships. For the purposes of the negotiation, you lot will be negotiating with me, Alice, Mattias, and other representatives from Produktion Group who are not with us this morning."

"For today," Mattias interjected, "we will have our breakfast here and then move to our office a few kilometers away to discuss the details of the transaction. Most of you are already aware, but please be advised that there should not be any discussion at our offices of the underlying subject of this transaction. To move quickly and effectively, we have limited disclosure of our intentions to those who must know in order to carry out our purpose. Those people are around this table now."

Michael filled his coffee cup from the carafe on the table, wondering whether Alice or Emil was Swedish intelligence. He had the sense that everyone was lying to some extent but that everyone also understood as much.

Oleg remained silent. Bits of melon lingered on his plate. He hardly touched anything else, as if the conversation was filling enough. He sipped his coffee like he had an ulcer, wincing each time.

"There is an old proverb: 'the seller has one price and the buyer quite another,'" Alexei said, drawing the attention of the Swedes, who waited for Alexei to continue before responding. "Tell me, Mattias, have you truly come to understand what the price is here?"

Mattias shifted in his chair and gazed thoughtfully at a corner of the room for a moment. "We understand, Alexei. To illustrate, let me ask you something: do you think Sweden's C-Bureau adhered to the formal policy of neutrality or waited for approval of operations from the conservative government? The answer is *no*. They did not wait for the political winds of the day to blow in their direction. They took action."

Mattias looked to everyone at the table with a cool sincerity. "Today, Sweden is sending billions of kronor in aide to Ukraine. It also provides training and equipment. Our nation has decided there is no possibility of neutrality. However, this is not enough. Typically, the government has no indication of where its funds or equipment is going. It lacks control, and the aid system is chaos." He continued on in a hushed tone, leaning in towards the table. "Blue Scepter is expanding, yet it struggles to get proper resources. We are looking for a concentrated effort to provide funding to this specific brigade, which will, in turn, use the funds to offer contracts to qualified—mostly American—volunteers." He spoke only to Alexei. "You ask of the price we pay...I will tell you that the price of pursuing this plan is a small one compared to what could happen if Ukraine does not win this war."

13

On the steps of the Grand Hotel, a gust of Saltsjön bay wind blew guests backward as they exited. The taxi-van driver wore a puffer coat and Gore-Tex gloves. A jangly Swedish advertisement played over the radio. Michael, Alexei, and Oleg sat crammed in the back seats as they drove through windy roads and old brick alleyways to a yellow plaster building with a green, zinc roof.

The large wooden doors opened with a slight pull of the frigid brass handle, revealing a small lobby with a lift and staircase to the right and what appeared to be a shut-down cafe to the left. Produktion Group's offices were on the second and third floors. They walked up the stairs to the third, where Mattias was waiting to escort them to the conference room. Emil and Alice sat at a glass-top table on top of a lime green rug. The floors were lightly colored wood and the hot-water radiators attached to the wall were beginning to clank as the boiler tried to keep up. The ends of branches from a nearby tree scratched the windowpanes like nails from a witch's crooked fingers.

There were two others sitting next to Emil and Alice, whom Mattias introduced as Johan and Tuva. Johan had dark hair and wore navy dress pants with a grey sweater over a shirt and tie. Grey and pink striped socks appeared at his ankles. Tuva looked young enough to be a recent graduate student and wore a light blue long-sleeve top with dark dress pants. A small painting of a coat of arms in a thick wooden frame hung on the wall; it depicted a knight's helmet on top of a shield, and within the shield was an illustration of two elk locking their antlers together in challenge. "Von" appeared in a flowing hand in the upper left corner of the painting and "Andersson" in the upper right. Michael stared at it as the branches continued to claw at the window.

Mattias offered the official backstory of the transaction, the necessity of obtaining the goods from Alexei's company, and time sensitiveness of the matter. He paced calmly around the room as he addressed everyone but was focused on the Produktion Group representatives, who sat quietly and took occasional notes on the pads in front of them. These were custom goods, and the specifica-tions had been agreed upon. Alexei was nearly the only man that could provide this specific of a good, and there would likely be more orders on their way. When Mattias finished, Johan asked Mattias whether Alexei and his colleagues were provided the terms and conditions of sale for review prior to the meeting.

"We have reviewed," Michael offered, opening the file in front of him and taking his gaze away from the coat of arms. The room seemed smaller than he imagined, and the negotiation appeared more routine to Emil and Tuva than he was anticipating. "We can largely accept your terms, except we have identified several items that we'd request to change, beginning with payment terms."

"This is music to our ears, isn't it, Tuva?" Emil replied. The others nodded approvingly and located the payment terms language to follow along.

"The issue," Michael continued, "is that this language makes for an uncertain timeline for payment, over which the Seller lacks control. As written, the time for payment is triggered after the invoice and goods are 'deemed satisfactory' in Buyer's sole discre-tion. I believe the parties have agreed on net forty-five payment terms, so we'd request to revise this language to provide that payment will be due forty-five days from the *date of the invoice*, which will be provided when the goods depart Alexei's factory."

"And what if the goods are defective or not acceptable?" asked Johan.

"There is a strong warranty provision included in your terms as well as inspection procedures, so this should cover you in the event of a defect or non-conformity. We think that situation is separate from the overall obligation to pay."

"Where is payment to be sent? And will it be in Swedish Kronor or US Dollar?" Tuva asked.

"Payment will be made in US Dollars to Seller's bank account in the US," Oleg replied in a tone that did not match the conversation. The window shutters fluttered outside as a breeze nestled its way through the alley.

"Oleg is correct, and we've brought a draft letter of credit that our bank provided which can be used to facilitate payment from Produktion Group's bank," added Michael, handing out copies of the letter of credit. The radiator clanked again over the silence as the one-page document was scrutinized around the table.

"We can likely use this, and the payment terms you request shouldn't be an issue," Tuva said, "but our bank typically requires sellers in similar international transactions to sign a short indemnification declaration providing that any funds that are seized by authorities must be reimbursed by the seller. We are not contemplating sending any goods or payment to a country that is subject to sanctions, it is just the US and Sweden, so the confiscation of funds should not be an issue."

"Michael, at what point in the transaction could this sort of confiscation by authorities occur?" Alexei asked.

"I agree with Tuva that it could arise if the Swedish or American government flagged goods or payment being sent to a country or person that is on a list of prohibited parties or a sanctions list," Michael paused, then added, "Funds could also be confiscated if

Produktion Group obtained the funds through illegal activity, in which case we would be responsible for reimbursing the bank."

"Oh, the vileness," Alexei said, as he leaned back in his chair and placed a hand on Mattias' shoulder. "I suppose we'll just have to take their word for it," he continued, "but maybe meet us...halfway...and we can each agree to reimburse the bank if anything happens to the payment?"

"The bank shouldn't mind if both parties are offering to reimburse it in the event payment is seized by a government," Michael added.

"I think that is reasonable, gents. Let us discuss it, and in the meantime, is there anything else we need to do with the letter?" Mattias asked. His question was directed at Tuva and Emil.

"I will scan a copy and then send it to our bank for their approval. I can also ask about both parties signing the indemnification declaration if that's what you wish," Tuva said.

"They should be able to respond within the next hour or two," added Emil. The door creaked open and a small cart carrying a samovar was rolled into the room.

"Please help yourself to a cup of coffee," Mattias said, motioning towards the samovar. "We will have a fika break now. I'm going to see if we can turn the heat down in this room. The radiators are blasting."

Mattias rose, pushed in his seat, and excused himself. Oleg sat with his hands folded in front of him as several others retrieved coffee. He took the cell phone out of his coat pocket that was hung on his seat, placed it in his front pocket, and exited the room in the opposite direction as Mattias with his coat tucked under his arm. Michael followed.

14

It was six o'clock in the morning and silent except for the sound of ice shattering outside Sue's window as a neighbor struggled to scrape a car windshield. By the sound of the stubborn ice, she estimated it was near or below zero degrees. She located her scrubs, guided only by the glow of snow and moon coming through the window, and dressed quickly after shedding her robe.

Her heart sank at the sound of the knock at the door, and the warmth of blood rose to the surface in her arms and face. The hallway motion light was triggered. Shadows of figures appeared beneath the door, a florescent light leaking in behind them.

Through the peephole, she saw Kristelena and Nikolai standing a foot away. Kristelena flipped her hair out from the inside of her long down jacket. Nikolai blew into his hands and rubbed them together. Sue opened the door, and light beat back the dim winter glow.

"Yes, everything is fine," Kristelena said. "Sorry it's so early, we wanted to catch you before we all went to work." She did not move from her place on the doorstep.

"Have you heard anything from Michael?" Sue asked. "I have a call scheduled with him later today."

"No, we were wondering if you had any news from him on how things are going on the trip."

"It sounds like it's going well. I know they had an important day today."

"They are meeting with the Swedish buyer today. We aren't concerned about them. Have you ever met Oleg?" Kristelena asked.

"No."

"He works with Alexei, Michael's client. He's Russian, like us. Alexei is Ukrainian. We met him through Alexei a few months ago, and Alexei vouched for him. Over the past few days, we've started having concerns."

"What kind of concerns?"

"Whether he has a different plan than the rest of us."

"We don't trust him," Nikolai said.

"Why's that?" Sue asked. She stood in the doorway, leaning against the door frame with her arms folded.

"One of our friends in Ukraine sent us a message about him. They said he talks to Russians," Nikolai said.

"But you're Russian," Sue said, looking each of them in the eyes. It wasn't a question; it was a statement which invited them to clarify or get out of her entry way.

"It's the kind we don't talk to, the kind we avoid at all costs," Kristelena said. Her voice was so low, Sue struggled to make the words out.

Sue leaned forward and whispered, "What do you want from us?"

"We want to keep you safe. You're on our side, and we protect each other. Have you seen anyone hanging out around here that you don't normally see? Any cars?"

"I'm not sure whose side I'm on," Sue said.

"Yes, Sue, you are. There are only two sides. You know which one you're not on," Kristelena said. Her palms were open, arms hung down by her sides. She wasn't whispering but her words were somehow quieter than a whisper. Her hazel eyes were still and focused on Sue, focused on this moment between the two of them.

"I haven't heard anything about Oleg from Michael or anyone else," Sue said. "I've never met him and hope I never do. I haven't noticed any people or cars hanging around, either."

"If you see a silver Honda Civic, license plate GPU 446, call us on this phone," Nikolai said. He handed Sue a burner phone. It was a cold little brick. "We're at the only number in the contacts."

"Who is in this car?" Sue asked.

"No one you should ever meet or hope to meet," Kristelena said. "We think the guy driving this car has been following us. Of course, we were careful not to bring him here. A couple of days ago, he followed us to the blood clinic where we sell our plasma. He asked a few questions at the front desk to pretend like he was interested in giving blood and then waited outside for us to leave."

"Why do you think he might want to follow me?" Sue asked.

Nikolai took a step back and leaned his shoulders and head against the wall behind him. He looked back at Sue and shrugged. "Michael."

"Is he Russian? Do you think he's involved with Oleg?" Sue asked.

"He didn't seem Russian, but he could be. Don't make that assumption. Mainly, we think he is working with Oleg and the Russians because we received his picture from our Ukrainian contact before we saw him in the US. Our friend warned us that this is someone Oleg is working with. Here is his picture. Look at it, but we can't give you a copy," Kristelena said.

The photo was zoomed in and showed a man sitting at a cafe table. He had salt and pepper hair, a thick build, and appeared to be in his early fifties. Sue handed the photo back to Kristelena.

"I still don't understand what this man would want from me," Sue said.

A ship horn thundered across the lake as Sue held the phone to her ear. It rang four times before Michael answered.

"I'm at the buyer's office," Michael said.

"Nikolai and Kristelena were just here. Is anyone around you?"

"No, I'm just walking down a stairwell. Oleg is ahead of me."

"He is with you still?"

"Yes."

"Kristelena and Nikolai said that they don't trust him. They said he might be working with the Russians. Someone in Ukraine told them." She spoke in a rush. Her hand shook as she held the phone to her ear. The ship horn thundered lowly. She looked out the window to see if the Volvo was gone.

"Slow down...they said Oleg was working with the Russians? As in the Russian government?"

"They didn't specify. They just said they have concerns about him, that he has a different plan than everyone else, and that the Russians that he's talking to are a problem. They are being followed by one of his people as well, and they told me to watch out for him. And, Michael, I can't do this. Please come home."

Michael reached the door to outside, opened it slightly, and saw Oleg on the corner of the street smoking a cigarette and mumbling into his cell phone.

"Do we need to get away from Oleg?" Michael whispered.

"Yes, don't confront him. I think you should just leave."

"I can't leave in the middle of the negotiation. It'd only draw attention. Who was following them?"

"Someone in a silver Honda Civic. I saw a picture. He had salt and peppery hair...older guy. Not sure if he's even Russian."

Michael shut the door to outside and turned back to the stairwell. He was thinking clearer due to the cool air or because he had to.

"Call the police if you see him," Michael said.

"Nikolai gave me a phone and said to call him if I think I'm being followed."

"I'd call Nikolai first."

15

"And now that your bank is satisfied with our solution, we can simply attach the letter of credit form to the order and it can be filled out upon booking," Michael said. Cups and plates with half-eaten rolls littered the table. It was no cooler in the room than before Mattias left to address the heat. Faces around the table were flushed. Water pitchers were empty, and the window glass was starting to cloud.

"Perhaps people should always negotiate in a room this stifling," Alexei said. He was perspiring more than anyone and wiped his brow with a black and white polka dot handkerchief.

They recovered by having lunch at the Grand Hotel. Michael, Alexei, and Oleg sat along a window wall in a room called the Veranda. It looked over the street, palace, and waterfront. Every ship in the bay was docked. Some boats were wooden and seaworn, some were glossy white yachts of the type used for Stockholm's corporate parties. The table had a bright white tablecloth, and the floor was creamy white tile. A crystal chandelier hung above them. Michael peered into the bowl of fish stew in front of him, measuring a spoonful.

"Michael," Oleg began, "have you set up the additional entities and bank accounts yet?"

"No, I'll do that when we get back to the US." He only lifted his head from the stew when he was done talking. He met Oleg's gaze and held it firmly.

"How long will that take?" Oleg asked.

"It will only take about two business days. There's plenty of time."

Oleg tossed his napkin on the table in annoyance and tucked his lips to one side for a moment. "This is going to move quickly, and we have to make sure we're ready."

"Actually," Alexei began, "I want to transfer the funds to a Swiss account that is in my name. I already have a banker advising me on this. There is no rush on the new US entities or accounts at this point."

"You want to take this money out of the country?" asked Oleg.

"It's going out of the country eventually...what's the difference?"

"Michael, excuse yourself for a few moments, please," Oleg said. His voice was steady and remained at the same level, like a bureaucrat directing a line of citizens at a government office.

"Michael will stay here," Alexei said.

Michael was motionless in his seat. He looked at his Longines, pretending to read the time, and took a deep breath. "Alexei, I can give you a minute."

"It's not necessary, Michael. We are protected by attorney-client privilege between us. Oleg is perhaps going to say that we planned to transfer some funds to certain ex-military Americans within the US as a direct inducement to fight with Ukraine, potentially in violation of US law."

"Precisely," Oleg said. He made a gesture with both hands and then set them down gently. He tapped his index finger softly on the tablecloth. "Hundreds of thousands of dollars ...to specific individuals who have been identified and contacted. Why the change?"

"Let's say that another donor has entered the picture, making it unnecessary for us, this time around, to make payments domestically. The same individuals and organizations are still in play. It's an...evolving situation. I will keep you informed, Oleg, and we still have work to do. For now, let's drop it. *Vy ponimaete*?"

"You should have told me earlier. I've been making arrangements."

"I only found out today, Oleg." Alexei sat back in his chair, leaning to one side with his arms folded over his broad chest. He looked out at the waterfront with serenity. "Let's go out tonight," Alexei added. "All we have done is work and live in this hotel. I feel like the *Gentleman in Moscow*, confined in a luxurious prison. At least the Metropol had music. We need to go where there is music. Even better if there are women. Even better still if they are Swedish women. My friend, Kirill, owns a club in Stockholm, in Södermalm. I will call him and see what is happening tonight. You see, Michael, an old goat like me must know the owner in order to get in anywhere."

"I think I'll stay in tonight, Alexei. There's a flight tomorrow morning that I'd like to catch," Michael said. He broke apart a piece of crisp bread and the crumbs flung across the table.

"Nonsense, Michael. You're young! And control yourself," Alexei said, brushing crisp crumbs onto the tile below. "Come and enjoy yourself. I'm sure you will make your flight. We won't be out too late. Like I said, I'm an old goat. Maybe you want to stay up all night so that you can sleep on the plane, though, eh?" Alexei winked at Michael and took a sip of his white wine. As he did so, he noticed the chandelier and took a moment to observe it.

"Oleg, *vy spite*? You sleeping? Coming along then?" Alexei asked.

Outside of the Veranda dining room, Oleg and Alexei walked ahead like two schoolboys skipping class. Alexei had his right arm over Oleg's shoulders and whispered something into his ear, followed by a deep, muffled laughing fit. Oleg's thin lips parted with a slight grin as he nodded along. The two almost knocked over a blue and white porcelain flower vase sitting on a table in the middle of the lobby. Oleg continued out the revolving front door as he slid his arms through the sleeves of his grey peacoat. He looked back at the lobby over his shoulder and met Michael's stare. Oleg rolled his steely eyes and walked on, no longer grinning.

Michael stood with Alexei and watched Oleg exit. Alexei picked up a newspaper from the lobby table and held it in front of him, but his eyes scanned the cars and people in front of the hotel.

"Do you know about Oleg?" Michael asked.

"Of course," Alexei replied. His eyes dropped down to the newspaper, a copy of the *Financial Times*.

"Who has he been talking to?"

Alexei's eyes were still on the newspaper. "We believe...*he* is with the GRU, Russian intelligence."

"I'm leaving," Michael said.

Alexei looked up at the street once more, saw Oleg get into a taxi, and then turned to Michael. "I'm afraid that may let him know something is off. We need him to come to the club tonight, and we need you to stay close."

16

Kirill's night club was a drab, residential-looking building with a mansard roof. It sat underneath a graffitied bridge and was built long before the bridge was erected. Only streetlights cast their feeble glow in its direction. The small, private room where Alexei, Michael, and Oleg sat on sofa couches was two levels below the ground. It was illuminated by pink neon lights that hung in geometric shapes from the ceiling. A pale reddish hue filled the air. Walls rattled and drinks trembled on the cocktail table as bass thumped rhythmically from the dance floor above.

"I left Russia because there are too many clubs in St. Petersburg already," Kirill said from a chair opposite the sofa couches. He wore a red and black leather motorcross jacket and black jeans. His arm was wrapped around the shoulders of a woman wearing thick heeled boots and dark lipstick. She sat on the arm rest of Kirill's chair. "I thought about Italy, but it's the dark, cold places that love my kind of club. The Swedish Polisen keep their distance as well. I don't even need to pay them." Kirill snapped his fingers in the direction of the private room's bar. A bartender arrived with a tray of yellow-tinted cocktails, a lemon twist cast in each glass. "Please, have a round on me. Welcome, my friends," Kirill said. He put his hand over his heart and dipped his head in a way that suggested routine.

The bartender handed out cocktails, beginning with Oleg. After the drinks were distributed, Oleg's eyes followed the bartender back to the bar where he placed the empty tray in the sink. Oleg smelled his drink, scowled, and placed it on the floor beside his chair. "Forgive me," he announced, "I prefer vodka, and I see a nice bottle over there that we shall have, Kirill."

"How about for the next round, Oleg? We should respect our host's generosity," Alexei said.

Without responding, Oleg proceeded to walk behind the bar and take a bottle of Moskovskaya vodka from the shelf. With his free hand, he handed two hundred US dollars to the bartender and took hold of three lowball glasses by pinching them between his fingers. He called for the bartender to follow him with three more glasses to the table, where he poured out six shots into the glasses, including one for the bartender. Alexei raised his glass, announcing, "na zdorovye".

From the private room, they climbed a spiral staircase and opened a metal door to a burst of echoing electronic music. Beams of blue and green shot out erratically from the stage and ceiling, and clouds of fog crept through the crowd. One of Kirill's security guards unhooked a velvet rope from the VIP section, and they followed Kirill inside. Before Oleg could enter, a young woman in a low-cut top and smoke colored eyes approached him. She pulled his jacket in the direction of the dance floor. He resisted her attempts and continued following the group.

"You wouldn't even with me?" she asked, speaking into his ear slowly over the sound of the music.

"Take my friend, Michael, here, I'm sure he would love to dance with you," Oleg said.

She frowned and put her hands on her hips. Oleg gave no response, so she lunged at him playfully and gripped the lapels of his jacket. She flipped her auburn hair in his face and looked at him with pouty lips.

"I'm sorry to disappoint," Oleg said.

"Take them both," Alexei said. "What is your name, lovely?"

"Alva, and you should all come out."

"We accept. Take both of them for now, the rest of us need to get our courage up," Alexei said.

"Both of us?" Michael asked.

Alexei rose from the couch where he had already sat and put an arm around Michael. "Yes, take them both." He gave Michael a pat on the back. While Alva drew Oleg's attention, Alexei leaned into Michael's ear. "Go with and leave them alone."

Alva took Oleg and Michael by the hand and led them away. She held Michael's with only a few fingers, as she clasped a lipstick case in the same hand. In the crowd, she let go of Michael's hand and twirled herself under Oleg's, continuing into the mass of people with him. Oleg watched Alva's black and white checkered skirt as he followed closely behind. Michael stood shoulder to shoulder with others but only moved to the extent they jolted him back and forth to the hypnotic pulsing of the music. He saw Alva and Oleg in frames through flashes of light. Her arms rested gently on his shoulders. Now she held him firmly around the neck with one hand and held his body tight to her with the other. Michael looked closer. They faded. In the next illuminated frame, Oleg broke from her grasp and stumbled backward in confusion, searching around. He took a step toward Alva and Michael weaved his way through to them. Alva stepped forward, pinning Oleg's arms to his waist and pressing herself against him. Oleg freed his arm and brought it back to swing as Alva struggled to get her arms around him. Closing in, Michael sprang forward and restrained him. Oleg resisted for a moment, then, to Michael's surprise, weakened. His mouth and throat struggled as if he was gulping down ink. Alva worked to support his weight. She put one of Oleg's arms over her shoulders and Michael, out of reflex, did the same. Oleg's breathing was labored, and he loosened the collar around his neck.

When they staggered out of the crowd, two security guards seized Oleg under the arms and rushed him to the stairwell. The toes of his black leather shoes danced on the sticky floor and dragged as they escorted him away. Michael turned to Alva in disbelief and saw her silhouette in a beam of blue as she faded into a sea of people. She vanished a moment later.

Michael's chest heaved as he moved farther from the dance floor. Alexei motioned for him and his vision focused. A group of young club goers with glowing necklaces brushed past on each side of him. One of them bounced off, and he realized he gave the man a stiff shoulder. He apologized briefly and walked to Alexei, who exited the VIP area where Kirill and his girl sat on a Victorian couch.

"What the fuck just happened?" Michael asked.

"It's done."

"What does that mean?"

"Come." Alexei motioned for Michael to follow him through the metal door and back down the spiral staircase.

"I'm not going back down there," Michael said.

"We can't talk here. Please come." They collected themselves on the gridded stairway landing.

"Tell me right now or I'm going up those stairs and you'll never see me again."

"I'll tell you downstairs."

Michael took a stride toward the upper staircase and Alexei placed a hand on the back of his shoulder. Alexei looked up and down the stairwell and saw no one. He stepped back, drew a breath in, and placed both his hands on the steel railing of the landing.

"He was working with the GRU, Michael. He had to go before one of us got hurt or he made a mess of everything." He released his grip on the railing and looked at Michael. "It had to be done."

His voice caught a note of low raspiness. It may have been his version of a whisper.

"Is he dead?" Michael asked.

"He should be soon." Alexei turned in place, facing Michael with his back to the railing.

"How?"

Alexei looked around again and saw no one. He looked at Michael with a wrinkled forehead and raised eyebrows. "She poisoned him."

"With what? Was his drink poisoned?"

"Yes, but he didn't drink it." Alexei felt the inside of his coat for his cigarettes and pulled one from the pack. He held it between his fingers unlit. "Alva did it with her lipstick. It is a pneumatic device and can inject poison. In this case, it was mostly a combination of ricin and aflatoxin. A medical examiner will find death by natural causes, specifically to the liver and kidneys." He lit the cigarette.

"Why was that necessary? Did you arrange for that to happen?"

Alexei exhaled a cloud of smoke that drifted up the stairwell. "Michael, we confirmed he was working for the GRU. We have pictures of him meeting with other, known, GRU agents. Oleg knew us, he knew you, and he knew your family."

"Even if he was a GRU agent, I don't understand this. It will bring more trouble on us if a GRU agent is killed."

"Us? Tonight was a Swedish intelligence operation, Michael. They received the information and made the call. They were protecting us. We don't have to worry now. We will be careful from here."

"Don't tell me recruiting soldiers from the west was Oleg's idea to begin with."

"No, it was the Ukrainians and Swedish Intelligence. Free East sent Oleg to assist. It shouldn't have happened. He was recommended by someone we believe was compromised by blackmail."

"And what about the man in the silver Honda following Nikolai and Kristelena?" Michael asked.

"They are paranoid. We have not confirmed this man is any kind of threat. Those two have been spooked twice before since arriving in the US."

"What if we see him around?"

"Then let us know and don't approach him."

"We'll be in the US. I would imagine the Swedes don't have anyone there. Even if they did, to be honest, I'm going to call the police if I see him. I'm going to tell Sue to do the same."

"To approach or call the police would do more harm than good. He has maybe crossed paths with Nikolai and Kristelena more than once, okay, fine, but probably on his way home from work. He's not a threat. Oleg was. It's done."

"Tell me why the GRU has even tried to get involved with your deal."

"This is what they do; they cast out their lackeys, like Oleg, or pay money to anyone stupid enough to get into bed with them, and they use them to sabotage anything that's against their interests. It's even better if they can steal while they're at it, funding their efforts with the money of their enemies." Alexei held his fingers out to count. "My best guess is, number one, Oleg planned to steal money from our transactions, number two, he intended to cut off recruits from their salaries, and number three, the GRU would have used the incident as a means to discredit the Ukrainian military in the minds of potential recruits from the west. There is already a propaganda war going on to dissuade foreign volunteers."

"I'm surprised you got this far with Oleg," Michael said. He looked through the metal grid under their feet and the winding staircase below it. "But here we are. Are you sure there isn't anyone else?"

"No." He waved a hand in the air as if warding off a ghost. The end of a burnt down cigarette smoldered between his fingers.

17

Early the next morning, Michael yawned as he walked from the checkout desk through the lobby of the Grand Hotel in his Red Wing boots. He had not slept well, repetitively replaying the scene of Oleg silently choking as he was carried out of the club. Twenty yards away, Alexei and Mattias gathered around a stone pillar. Mattias leaned against it with one hand on his hip. The navy-blue Lange & Söhne peeked out from under the sleeve of his overcoat. He bit his bottom lip, and his eyes focused on Alexei, whose skin had a pinkish flush that may have been brought on by the cold morning air. Alexei's scarf hung loosely around his neck.

Michael took heavy steps over to them. The soft carpet of the lobby absorbed the sound of his feet. He was about to announce his presence when Mattias said, "We don't know where he is."

"Who?" Michael asked.

"Oleg." Mattias glanced down at Michael's Longines. "You like the watch?"

Michael stared back at both of them, trying not to ask the questions that swirled through his mind.

The lobby doors opened. A gust of cool, sea air struck them.

The smell of jasmine perfume emanated from a group of new guests.

Alexei snapped a look to Mattias. "I thought this was under control, Mattias. We have a man who is working with—" He stopped himself mid-sentence and started again. "We have a man we both know is a concern, and now you are telling me your service has lost him? That he is God knows where?"

"We had people stationed at this hotel all night. He has not been back here."

"What do you mean? I thought he was dead. Where did he go?" Michael asked.

"We don't know where he is, but the intent was never to keep him as a prisoner," Mattias said. "The guards at the club escorted him outside. They had no idea what was going on." Mattias paused as the perfumed guests passed. Alexei took his leather gloves off and adjusted his scarf, throwing the tail of it over his shoulder.

"We're lucky no one else got hurt," Mattias said. "Oleg had a blade strapped to his ankle. He may have pulled it on Alva if Michael hadn't stepped in. He tried to pull it on the guards outside the club. They took it away and let him go."

"We should have made sure to end him right there in that dirty little club," Alexei said.

"That would have complicated things," Mattias said. "This way, he is removed as a threat with minimal fallout. These days, people think the Russians are the only ones capable of doing a hit with poison. If anything ever leaked, it would be easy to say the Russians were taking out one of their own abroad, as they have done before."

"Was this anticipated?" Michael asked.

"They tell me it can be a while before the mixture fully takes effect, sometimes a few days or more than a week," Mattias said. "They say the end result is inevitable. He likely jumped on a plane and is heading back to Russia if he is still alive. We will probably hear one way or another soon."

"What if he has fallen dead on the side of a Stockholm road?" Michael asked.

"Then that is what happens, and it's not your problem. That is a Swedish matter. As I've told Alexei and he has told you, any investigation would indicate a death by natural causes. Our service will suppress any formal investigation."

Alexei stood with his hands together in front of him, gripping his gloves, his knuckles whitening. "Mattias will lean on his contacts to eliminate trails back to Kirill's club."

Out of the corner of his eye, Michael saw a figure burst through the front door of the lobby. Emil strode towards them. His cheeks were rose-tinted. His long brown overcoat unbuttoned, fluttering behind him. "We found him," Emil said. "He's in the hospital."

———

Michael stood over a plastic sack of brass bullet cartridges on the Brower & Wood conference table. The woman who waited for his reaction had a thin manilla file under her arm. Her hair was pulled back in a low, sleek ponytail. She glared at him from behind her thin-framed glasses.

"Agent Pallows, I'm not sure what I'm looking at," Michael said.

"This is a sample of physical evidence from our investigation involving Alexei Stakhanovich."

"An investigation by the Bureau of Alcohol, Tobacco, Firearms, and Explosives?"

"Yes, and we will be coordinating with the FBI based on Alexei's most recent plans. You got in last night from Stockholm. Is that right, Michael?"

"Yes, I landed in Minneapolis late afternoon and then drove home."

Michael adjusted the Longines around his wrist as if it was a shackle and sat down. "I'd be glad to help as much as I can, Agent Pallows."

"I'm glad to hear that. See, we think you've gotten in over your head and may not understand what is happening here. We think you can be a big asset to us at the ATF."

"Why have you taken an interest in Alexei?" Michael said. The words came from the back of his throat.

"It's not just him. He is part of a criminal enterprise." Agent Pallows opened the folder and slid a photo across the table. Her nails were bitten back. She remained standing.

"I know Nikolai," Michael said. He stared down at a photo of Nikolai walking to his Volvo.

"And her?"

The next photo was a close up of Kristelena sitting in the passenger seat of the car. She stared blankly out of the window with glumness.

"Yes."

"What's her name?"

"Kristelena."

"And how about this one?" Agent Pallows withdrew a photo of a middle-aged man standing outside of a sleepy, tin warehouse.

"I've never seen this one."

"Are you sure? Look at him." She gestured at the photo with a wave of her hand. She was like a mechanic indicating that an engine was obviously beyond repair.

"I'm sure. Who is it?"

"His name is Gregory Stepanov. I'm surprised you don't know him. He runs a dental practice and an import-export business out of Duluth. Nikolai and Kristelena live and work with Gregory."

"I've never met him. I knew about the dental practice and the import-export business, and I know Nikolai and Kristelena live with him. Are they under surveillance?"

Agent Pallows gathered the photos together and arranged them neatly in the file before closing it. The file was cheap and new. She paced around the room now with her back to him. "What do you know of the import-export business?"

"Not much. I think he does cars, pottery, and carpets. Nothing crazy as far as I know. I think he sells pottery on Etsy, at least that's what Nikolai told me."

"And can you explain, based on your understanding, the connection between Alexei Stakhannovich and these individuals?"

"Nikolai came to me and asked if I could help his friend, Alexei, with a business transaction, so I believe they are friends. I do not know of any connection between Alexei and Gregory or the import-export business."

"Tell us more about the transaction," Pallows said, though it was only her and Michael in the room. Pallows stood in front of the center window, the brackish morning sky visible behind her.

Michael studied her for a moment. "Could I see your badge, Agent Pallows?"

Pallows shrugged. "Of course." She opened a billfold and flashed her badge for a moment. Michael made out 'ATF' across the top.

"I don't feel comfortable providing more details on the transaction. Alexei is a client. The details of the transaction are privileged."

"Michael, this is a criminal investigation. There is no privilege under these circumstances."

"No privilege? You mean it's been waived somehow? I'm sorry, Agent Pallows, I'm going to need more information or a search warrant from you to speak further." Michael contracted his toes in his boots as he spoke. He hadn't thought about search warrants since taking the criminal law portion of the bar exam.

"Michael, there are also ethical factors to consider. You can't knowingly assist a client in criminal conduct."

Michael's eyes flared. "I have not engaged in that type of conduct. As is required, if anything was in the realm of criminality, I would have discussed the potential consequences and tried to counsel away from breaking the law. That would be my duty as counsel."

"I'm asking for your cooperation, Michael, please don't make this more complicated for yourself."

"I'm glad to cooperate, short of providing material that breaches my duty to Alexei. Besides, a wrongful seizure of material would jeopardize your investigation. We are all on the side of justice here. If this is a criminal matter, please consider me his defense counsel and call me when you have a warrant."

Pallows smiled with cold pleasure. "This would play out badly for you and your firm. You are currently aiding and abetting a criminal organization in the illegal distribution of weapons and support of a foreign military."

"Are these the allegations against Alexei?"

"We believe he is using his business to mask transactions involving guns and ammunitions and, more recently, recruitment activity in the US. He is using Gregory's import-export infrastructure for his operations."

"I've never seen any weapons or ammunition."

"Have you actually seen the products they are talking about?" Pallows asked.

Michael let the question pass without acknowledgment.

Pallows cleared her throat and crossed her arms. "It's not just information that we want from you; we want your active cooperation to take these people down. This would be beneficial for you. We aren't sure how Alexei is planning to move forward, or to what extent the Swedes are involved, but we have reason to believe he is ramping up operations for the purpose of illegally sponsoring Americans to serve in Ukraine."

"What would this active cooperation look like?"

"We need to follow the money."

"What type of evidence do you hope to find with this investigation?"

"We want tracing ability and names. That's where you come in. You will designate our account as the account to be used for Alexei's operation and pass on any details on potential transferees."

She handed him a document with a bank account and routing numbers. It had no official heading or language, only bullet points with the account information included in small font.

"You would want me to pursue this now?" Michael asked. "Time is of the utmost importance. I can come back with a search warrant from a judge and take your files, or you can give them to me and start cooperating with us."

"I'm not giving you my files."

She picked up the sack of bullet cartridges and placed it in an interior pocket of her black wool coat. "Keep those banking details and input them in your contracts when the time comes, and if you see any lists of recruits, please pass those along to us as well." She placed a business card on the table. It had nothing except a phone number scribbled in blue ink.

Michael rose from his seat. "I think that's it then," he said in Russian.

"I don't speak Russian," Pallows said.

"Lucky for you, it's an awful language to learn. Can I walk you out?"

"I will manage myself. Remember that there is a difficult way to do this and an easy way, Michael. They are using you. You don't need to protect them, no matter how much you like speaking Russian and traveling the world with them."

"I appreciate your concern, and I'll think about all of this." Michael extended his hand across the desk, but the moment lapsed, and he let his hand fall by his side.

"One more thing," Pallows said. "We'll get what we need with or without you." She put out her hand. It was cold, clammy, and fleeting.

John Sondheim read the *Duluth Tribune* at the reception counter in the lobby outside the conference room. After Pallows reached a safe distance away, Sondheim set the paper down. "Who was that?" he asked.

"Just met her, she's a concerned friend of a client." Michael turned into the hallway and began to run, knocking over a stack of books sitting on a stool outside the library as he rounded another corner. He reached the staff entrance and cracked the door open with a metallic screech. There was a row of parked cars. No Pallows. He heard tires crunching snow and slid out the door. Putting his hands on the cool brick facade, he peered around the side of the building and saw a rusted pick-up truck pass by. Now he saw Pallows walking, hunched, through an aisle of cars in the back of the lot. She pulled out her phone and made a call. Michael's fingers burned from the cold, and he placed them on the back of his neck to warm them.

A minute later, a silver Honda Civic sailed into the lot and turned towards the back row. Pallows got in the passenger seat. Michael memorized the license plate number. The car reversed and pulled away. Squinting, Michael spotted the back of the driver's head. There was enough light in the day to make out his salt and pepper hair.

18

Jagged plates of snow and ice rose, fell, and shattered among the waves. Through stinging eyes, Michael gazed at the lighthouse on the end of the breakwater. A frigid Superior mist lingered, smelling of wet stone. The concrete walls and steel light posts along the walkway were frosted over.

"Oleg is dead," Nikolai said.

"Is that why you brought me down here?" Michael asked. He fixed his squinted eyes on Nikolai now.

"I also wanted to show you something."

"What?"

"You'll see soon."

"How do you know Oleg is dead?" Michael asked.

"The Swedes called Alexei a few hours ago."

"I'm sure he's relieved."

Nikolai said, "Can a dead man feel relief? Maybe."

"Be serious."

"Alexei is relieved, and so is Mattias, as we all should be."

"What did Alexei say?" Michael asked, followed by his lawyer's head tilt.

"He's glad the Swedes are taking care of it. I can see you are stressed, Michael. It is for good reason, too. I mean, a man was killed. This does not happen every day. But Michael, believe me, the Swedes are capable of dealing with this. More than that, you are part of this world now, and you must learn to take things as they come."

"This isn't my world. I'm just a lawyer."

"Well, it is now, and there are plenty of lawyers who have given everything they have for this cause."

Michael digested Nikolai's candidness in silence, nodding occasionally. After a full minute of reflection as they both watched the waves, he asked, "Does Mattias' company know anything about Oleg?"

"No, and the transaction is moving forward."

"The Swedish intelligence service knows about Oleg since they were the ones who took him out. I'm curious why they would feel comfortable moving forward."

"They assessed the potential damage and aren't worried, even if he already reported everything he knew back to the Russians. He didn't know enough to throw us off course."

"He knew about all of us. Isn't that enough?" Michael asked.

"Join the club. You want to take a stand but remain in the shadows? Everyone who is truly making a difference in this struggle has their name on a list. It's a risk we are all willing to take. This is the reality of fighting against Putin's Russia."

Michael tore away, putting his hands at his sides. "I'm not helping with anything until we get some more things settled."

"We'll need you to set up those domestic bank accounts very soon."

"I thought Alexei was going to offshore the money from the transaction."

"He only said that to rattle Oleg. The money will be coming into his business account soon and we'll need to start the distribution process."

"Are you worried about law enforcement in the US?" Michael asked. "Is that why Alexei wants to set up additional accounts?"

"Weren't you saying that Alexei should put some distance between Minnesota Instruments and foreign transactions?" Nikolai asked.

"Yes, but not for the purpose of evading authorities."

"We're trying to fund a cause with legitimate money and keep it separate from Alexei's company. We're not laundering money, and we're not raising a military force in the US."

Michael stood six inches in front of Nikolai with his squinted eyes. They were nose to nose. "I understand that, and that's why I'm still here, but this is becoming more dire every day. Have you ever been approached by law enforcement?"

Nikolai looked at him squarely. "No."

"Alexei didn't think much of your follower in the silver Honda," Michael said. He paced gently around the icy concrete, placing his Red Wings down heel to toe, regaining feeling in his feet.

"He thinks it's nothing. Have you seen him around?" Nikolai asked.

Michael let the question drift by him as if Nikolai was a testifying witness who required no reply. He would not let Nikolai's question spoil his probing. It was a cross examination on the breakwater.

"Who do you think he is?" Michael asked, again with the lawyer's head tilt.

"Not someone we want around. I don't know who he is, but he's not with us," Nikolai said, placing his hand on his chest as he said 'us.'

Michael tucked his chin into his coat and breathed hot air against his collar. Nikolai looked back at him with a calm evenness.

"Is it possible that he is a federal agent?" Michael asked, leading him.

"It's possible, but unlikely." Nikolai studied the water, picking out one of the waves and following it until it struck the side of the concrete.

"What would you..." Michael stopped. He thought about walking off the breakwater to his car and never looking back. He remained still in his boots. "What would you think if I told you there's an investigation happening?"

"Again, I think that's unlikely. I wouldn't believe anyone unless they pulled me into a real federal office and maybe not even then."

"Why would I take that risk for you? For any of you?" Michael cast his hand out at the water, as if brushing away any possible explanations.

Up until this point, Nikolai allowed Michael space to move about. Now he leaned forward and put a hand on Michael's shoulder. "Because you believe in what we're doing, and you want to make a difference. Let's not lose focus."

Michael drew a breath in and held it for a moment until exhaling, the vapors forming a cloud that may have signaled his retreat. "Until I'm sitting inside a federal field office or served a judge's order, I'm going to believe you and try to see this through."

"Good. Do you want to tell me more about your worry of an investigation?"

A silver-toothed wave crashed against the wall, tossing scraps of ice at them over the barrier.

"Let's get out of here before we get taken out to sea," Michael said. His cotton hat was infused with young ice.

"Not yet," Nikolai said over the sound of the waves.

Michael drew in another breath and said, "I had a visitor early this morning."

"At work?"

"Yes, at the firm. She asked the secretary to call me down. Wouldn't give her a name at reception, just that she wanted to speak with me. We went into a conference room, and she closed the door behind us. I offered her a cup of coffee, and she tossed a bag of bullets on the table. She said it was evidence in an investigation that she and the ATF were doing."

"Bullets?"

"Big ones."

"She said she was an ATF agent?"

Michael nodded. "And that her name was Agent Pallows. She said you're all selling guns and ammunition among other things."

"I've never heard of her. Listen, I'm not saying she wasn't an agent, but I think there is a small chance we're being investigated by a federal agency. I'm not sure where those bullets would have come from. Maybe from us, who knows, but we aren't selling arms and ammunition. There's plenty of that in Ukraine already anyway."

"You're sure?"

"Of course, I'll take you to Gregory's shop or anywhere else you want to go."

"She had a badge. I didn't get a close look."

"Do you want me to take you to Gregory's shop to get this idea that he is running guns out of your head?"

"No, it's okay. Here's the thing, I ran to the staff entrance and watched her leave. She got picked up by a guy in a silver Honda. He had salt and peppery hair. That's how Sue described the guy who was following you."

"Michael, I think it's most likely that this person isn't who they say they are. She would have driven herself to your firm in a government vehicle and been open about being a federal agent with others at your firm, maybe talked to your boss. She didn't talk to anyone else?"

"Just to me."

"Did she leave contact information?"

"Just a card with a phone number written in pen."

"Forget her. I'll talk to Alexei about it. Did you happen to catch the license plate number?"

"It was GPU 4463."

"That's the car," Nikolai said. He glanced back at the parking lot on the pier. "Do you know if anyone was following you here?"

"I didn't see anyone behind me, and I did two laps around before parking. No one comes out here in January, it would have been obvious if anyone was behind me. Why are you smiling?"

"You're good at this, Michael. Also, I can't wait to tell Alexei he was wrong."

"About me?"

"About the car. He knew you had some grit after the club in Stockholm."

"Pallows gave me some bank account numbers and wanted me to put them into the contracts."

"I think she's filling in for Oleg. If they get their hands on this money, it will be a massive blow to Blue Scepter and the operation."

"The Ukrainian Brigade?"

"Yes, the Russians are doing everything they can to undermine its ties to the west."

"Pallows said she didn't speak Russian."

"She doesn't have to speak Russian. Money is a worldwide language, so is blackmail."

"You think she was either paid to impersonate an agent or she is an agent and is being blackmailed?"

"Anything is possible. Ever heard of Charles McGonigal, Robert Hanssen? And they were high profile FBI agents. Do what you think is right, Michael, but I would say don't believe a damned thing."

"I told her I'd need to see a warrant before providing any information."

"I want you and Sue to be safe," Nikolai said in Russian. "I think we're the best people to protect you right. For now, let's keep moving forward. We'll proceed carefully."

A charcoal-colored freighter glided out of the fog. It had three deck cranes and scrapes like claw marks running along its side. Its crevasses seemed to ooze a dark and bitter molasses. The ship horn rang, its rumbling tone cutting through the cold.

"This is what I wanted to show you."

"The ship?"

"It's from the Swedes. Don't mind the Panamanian flag. It's a flag of convenience."

"Coming to pick up the goods? I thought we were doing air freight."

"No, not for the goods. This ship is coming from Mattias' government friends."

"What's it doing here?"

"It's stopping here briefly on its way to the Black Sea." Nikolai placed his hands on the edge of the wall. "You see, it's picking up some American passengers for its voyage. They happen to be veterans of the US Special Forces."

"You mean, they are recruits," Michael said.

"They were promised nice sums of money upon arrival."

"By Alexei?"

"By Blue Scepter. Alexei's money is flowing through Free East to Blue Scepter. The Ukrainians worked their magic on the internet to attract talented recruits. Alexei has arranged for them to get passage on the ship."

"Are you crazy? It's January. Winter came late this year, but the Soo Locks will shut down for repairs any day. No salties can go through after that."

"What's a saltie?" Nikolai asked.

"A ship that travels the ocean."

"It will not be a problem, there are still several ships departing over the next week or so."

"If it's the last one, it'll be all over the news," Michael said. "There's fanfare for the last saltie that goes out. This doesn't look like a military ship. Is it?"

"Of course not, it's a merchant vessel. They will outfit it with deck guns and speed boats when it gets to Odessa."

"Why are the Swedes offering this?"

"What do you know of Russia's ghost fleet?"

Michael put a hand to his forehead. He took his hat off and shook the ice crystals loose. "How is that relevant? I don't know, Nikolai, they use ships from other nations to transport oil and get around western sanctions. It funds Russia's war effort."

"Yes, but they also have surveillance equipment and are used for sabotage, such as cutting power cables under the sea floor," Nikolai explained. "Like this ship, they are registered with a foreign nation to cover up the ownership structure and deal with limited regulation. They are not obviously Russian ships. It could appear as a ship from Turkey, Panama, Liberia, Lithuania."

"So, the Swedes got their own ghost ship?"

"They will sail under the flag of Panama through the Mediterranean as if a merchant ship. It will get its teeth in the Black Sea. Blue Scepter, with the help of our recruits and this ship, will target select vessels and shipping companies that are acting as agents of Russia. These targets are believed to be connected with Russian activity around the world, including in the Baltic."

"When do they sail?"

"In a couple days. Before then, it's critical that the Russians do not find out the identity of this ship or its plans."

19

"I've barely seen you these last few weeks," Sue said. She combed her hair, looking at Michael in the bathroom mirror. He wondered why she didn't face him directly to speak but realized he had been fussing with one thing and then another since he got home. One moment he was working on his laptop, the next he was throwing clothes in the wash, getting a glass of water, or even fixing the curtain rod in their bedroom. It could have been that *he* couldn't face *her*.

"I know, it'll be over soon." He stepped to her in the bathroom and draped his arms over her. His mind still raced, and he felt his stomach sway as if he had motion sickness. He held her tighter and raised his eyes to meet hers in the mirror, hoping that they would be kind.

They always were, and they were now. The motion sickness faded. Now, if he could just tell her everything. If she knew all, they could be reunited as one and face this new reality together as husband and wife. No, he thought. It was his mess. Things had gone too far to turn back. Most importantly, Nikolai was right: he still believed.

"Have you seen that Honda around?" Michael asked. He still hung his arms around her shoulders like the weight he hoped he wasn't.

"No. What was that about? It scared me when Nikolai and Kristelena came here. I thought they were going to tell me something happened to you, but then they started talking about being followed. They gave me that sketchy little phone to call them if I saw him. I called you." Her eyes were welling up. She dabbed at one of them with a finger.

"They don't know who he is, but I think they are right that he's following them. They aren't interested in you, though."

"What about you? Are they following you?"

"I don't think so," Michael said. He released her from his grasp. She turned to him.

"Have you seen him?"

"I haven't," he said, telling himself that he was protecting her.

"I think we should go to the police."

"Unless we're in immediate danger, there's nothing the police will be able to do for us, and it will make the whole thing more complicated."

"What whole thing?" Sue's eyes were dry now and pointed.

"The transaction," Michael said.

"This damn deal. What is it really about?"

"I'm learning gradually. I don't want to burden you with this. I can handle it."

"Tell me." She placed both her hands on his chest, as if summoning the truth from within him. Michael turned his back, and like a ballet dancer, Sue shifted with him, moving her hands up to his face and peering into him. And now Michael's eyes teared in the presence of her unconditional love.

"That was the last time you talked to Mattias?" Sue asked. Her head rested on the pillow beside Michael's.

"Yes, I told him I was done. I was just in for that one job," Michael said.

"Do Nikolai and Alexei know that he's your great uncle?"

"I'm not sure, maybe. They haven't said anything that makes me think they know."

"What did he do with the lists you gave him?"

"Swedish intelligence swallowed them up, probably flagged the companies on them, maybe more than that. There wasn't anything in the news. Apparently, things have gotten worse in the Baltic since then, so I'm not sure how much good it did."

"What convinced you to help him?" Sue asked.

"I'm half Swedish, and I'm a Swedish citizen. I felt I owed some loyalty. He's also family, and he gave me this speech about the things we've done to stand up against the injustice of other nations going back for generations. First against the Nazis, then against the communists. My grandpa's cash register business had a large presence in Europe, especially Germany. He was involved with several western intelligence operations that helped run agents in East Germany. I already knew all of it, but growing up here, it was all so distant to me. They were bedtime stories my mom would tell me. Fairytales. In a way, I felt my identity re-affirmed by helping him." Michael turned over and faced Sue. "I'm not a spy. It was just the one job. They never brought me formally in their service."

"Were you scared?"

"Beforehand, but when I sat in Hunt's office in the Embassy, I felt I couldn't afford to let it get to me. I just had something to get done. At that time, as Mattias explained to me, there was no certainty that the Americans would pass on this type of information to the Swedes, and it was important that they knew for their own security. My decision was already made."

"So you just reached into his brief case and found the list that Mattias was talking about?"

"We set it up so that my meeting followed his lunch with the Lithuanian who provided the information. It was a cold call for Hunt. I'm sure he didn't fully understand what it was or why it was given to him. The chances were high it would still be in his briefcase, and it was. When I left his office, he turned the other way down the hall, and I dove back in. I snapped a picture and ducked out."

Sue scratched the contours of her shoulder lightly as she listened. "When did you figure out Mattias was involved with Alexei's deal?"

"In the airport at MSP."

"Why did you still go?"

"In a way, it made me feel more comfortable that he was involved. I felt less on an island with what I was doing." Michael eased his eyes shut and sank with a breath deeper into the bed.

Sue brushed her fingers over his eyes. "And the ship leaves in a couple days? A saltie this time of year?"

Michael unsealed his tired eyes and focused them on Sue. "Yes, at four in the morning. It'll be one of the last salties out of the harbor for the season."

"That's cutting it close. Let's wait and see what this Pallows does. I imagine she'll follow up with you either way, whether she is who she says or if she's working for the Russians. Do you think she'll come back with a warrant?"

"No. Maybe it's just that I hope she's not, but I don't think she's with the ATF, just as I don't think the man in the Honda is with the ATF."

"Do you still trust Nikolai?"

"I know he's not telling me everything, but I think what he's told me is true. To be honest, I don't want to know everything."

"I think you should let this all go and be done with them."

"I still have to paper this deal. I think funding for the operation depends on it."

"Can't they do it themselves from here?"

"It's too risky. I want to do it and keep this as legitimate as possible. I don't want them handing out cash to some crew of mercenaries before they jump on a ship in the Duluth harbor. If they were recruited online by the Ukrainians and won't get paid until they arrive, that's a different story. I can live with that. If I drop out, there's no telling where things will go."

Sue rested her chin on his chest. "You'll find the right path through this. I know you will because I know you."

Michael's cell phone rang in the pocket of his pants, lying near the doorway. He slid out from the bed and stepped over to them, outside the glow of the bedside lamp.

"It's Alexei," he said. He stepped back into the lamp's soft light and looked at Sue as he took the call. Sue nodded and pulled the blankets over herself.

"I've heard about your day, Michael," Alexei said.

"Yeah? It was a busy one."

"Can you meet me tonight?"

"Sure, where?"

"Across the bridge, in Superior. The Northern Saloon. Twenty minutes."

Michael rang off. "He wants to meet me in Superior in twenty minutes. I better get going."

"He knows about everything today?"

"I'm guessing Nikolai told him. That's probably why he wants to meet outside of town. He didn't give any background on the phone, but he never does." Michael went to the closet and pulled on his jeans and thermal sweater.

"Maybe I should come with you," Sue said.

"No, it's okay. I want you involved in this as little as possible." They kissed and held it for a few moments. Michael turned for the door.

"Wait," Sue said. She put her hand out with his wallet. Michael reached for it, but she didn't let go. "You still have that movie ticket in there don't you?"

"Of course, it was our first date."

Sue let go of the wallet. "You've had that for ten years. You see, you're still you, Michael. You are who you always have been."

20

Through the dark, Michael followed the smoldering end of Alexei's cigarette to the doors of the saloon. Alexei stood in the cavernous doorway, surrounded by faltering wood panels.

"You were wrong about Nikolai's man," Michael said.

There were no windows, only a steel, red door under a dull beam of sickly yellow light. The finish on top of the handle was worn to a shiny chrome. The smell of cigarette smoke mixed with a scent of new paste, which could have recently been applied to the wood paneling.

Alexei stepped on his cigarette and swung his arm around Michael, leading him through the steel door. "So he told me. Come, come."

The bartender glanced sideways at them as he counted change out for a customer at the bar. Nikolai and Kristelena stood around a billiards table with a glass Budweiser lamp hanging above it.

"And I heard he has a woman." Alexei walked to the cue rack and withdrew two, handing Michael one of them with its glossy handle presented.

"You want to play, Michael? Nikolai and I will pool shark you," Kristelena said. She lined up the cue ball with a brief but intense focus and broke with a smack. "Russian balls are bigger, except for Nikolai's," she added with a wink and her closed mouth laugh.

"That's no way to treat a former lover," Nikolai said.

"Why am I here?" Michael asked. He set the cue against the table and put his hands in the front pockets of his Carhartt.

"We wanted to put your mind at ease," Alexei said. He moved to the table and pelted a corner pocket with a striped ball. "Have some beer if you'd like." Alexei pointed to a pitcher on a nearby high-top with the tip of his cue.

"No, thanks."

"Mattias and his friends do not believe this agent Pallows exists," Alexei said. "They have found no record of her. We just have to keep her, her escort, and her escort's shitty Honda at a distance, particularly until the Leamas sails."

"The Leamas?"

"The ship you saw calling at port today." Alexei lined up another shot with one eye squinted and sank it.

Another trace of Mattias' Le Carre obsession, Michael thought.

"How are we doing over here?" the bartender asked. He was a tall, skinny man with tarnished blue jeans, neatly combed grey hair, and a faded tattoo of a flaming skull on the inside of his right arm.

"Just fine, thank you," Alexei said.

"I haven't seen you all around here. Where are you from?" The man smiled and brushed his face with a few fingers as if he had walked through a cobweb.

"Europe," Alexei said. He raised his voice on the first syllable and tailed off, indicating that was the end of his explanation.

"Probably don't have many places like this saloon over there. Listen, finish your game, but there's a pool night about to start in fifteen minutes. They're going to need all of our tables." He motioned at the table in front of them and two more on the other side of the room that sat under unlit Budweiser lamps.

"We'll be done soon," Alexei said.

Alexei watched the bartender walk back to the bar as he chalked his cue and scanned the men playing pull tabs at the counter.

"We're not all from Europe," Michael said.

"You're Swedish, aren't you?" Alexei asked. "Mattias told me in Stockholm."

"You didn't know before?" Michael asked.

"No, why should I?"

"Because you already knew Mattias," Michael said. "He's my great uncle."

"I did not know that before, but I suppose it helps explain his trust in you," Alexei said. "He's the one who recommended we work with you."

"Why didn't you tell us before that Mattias is your uncle, Michael?" Nikolai asked.

"By the time I found out, I thought all of you may have known or weren't supposed to know," Michael said.

"I will have some more beer before we go," Nikolai said. He poured himself a glass. Most of it was foam.

"Did you know Mattias before, Nikolai? What about you, Kristelena?" Michael asked.

"Yes, but did not know that he was family," Nikolai said. "We looked into you after speaking with Mattias. He thought highly of you, that you stand up for what is right. We went along with Mattias' recommendation after that."

"Mattias did not want to make a direct approach to you for whatever reason," Alexei said.

"The reason was I told him I was done working with him," Michael said.

"What happened?" Kristelena asked.

"I did a job for him in Stockholm a few years ago. After that, I told him I couldn't be involved with his schemes anymore."

"Does he have a lot of schemes, your uncle?" Kristelena asked. She may have been amusing herself with the question.

"Everyone has a scheming uncle, don't they?" Alexei said. "He wanted you to see the merits of this mission before saying no."

"Hell, it worked."

"We are very close to finishing our portion of this, Michael. The recruits have arrived. However, they need some assurances. They need an American, a lawyer, to tell them how the plan is going to go."

"You mean they don't trust the online chat messaging that got them here?"

"No. Your input would give them confidence that payment will be made."

"You want me to go talk to them?"

"It will be a quick in and out," Nikolai said.

"It looks like the pool club is here," Michael said. A group of patrons gathered around the bar and started collecting pitchers of pre-poured beer. The lights above the other billiard tables flickered on. "I'm not going to give them certainty or some rah-rah speech."

"That's not what we're hoping for, just some comments on the arrangement," Nikolai said.

"When?" Michael asked.

"Tomorrow night, before the Leamas departs for the Black Sea," Nikolai said.

Kristelena returned her cue to the rack and picked up a tightly rolled brown paper bag. She handed it to Michael as if he was expecting to receive it and said, "for temporary protection."

Michael's hands balled up in his coat pockets. He took in their disinterested expressions and said, "I don't need anything."

"Just take it, you don't have to use it," Nikolai said.

Michael took the bag, unfurled it with caution, and peeked inside at the black Smith & Wesson handgun.

21

Alexei brushed the snow off the park bench with the leather gloves clenched in his hand. He groaned as he tucked his belly in and leaned over to set his steaming coffee cup down. The lamps along the pathway were still lit from the evening, though it was past nine in the morning. Fresh snow towered on the dead shrubbery, mocking it. In the distance off the shore, a fog crept in like coal smoke. Alexei cleared his throat of the January air.

Michael withdrew a sheet of paper from the file under his arm and passed it to Alexei. "These are the details for the new business entities and bank accounts." The paper crinkled in the lake breeze as Michael held it out. Alexei pulled his gloves on before accepting the document, as if adding another layer of protection by not touching it with his bare fingers.

"Excellent," Alexei said. His eyes shifted from left to right as he pored over its contents. "We received full payment on the letter of credit already," he said as he continued to read. "We won't have much time to transfer the funds through these accounts abroad."

"Who should I tell the recruits is paying them? Blue Scepter?"

"We send to Free East, Free East sends to Blue Scepter, and Blue Scepter pays the recruits. There is no need to tell the recruits about the chain of funds, just that they will be paid by Blue Scepter. Do you have the account information that Pallows provided?"

Michael reached into the pocket of his Carhartt and produced a small, evenly folded square. He held it out between his fingers. "Is there a way to see who owns these accounts?"

"I will pass it along to Mattias. The Swedes can trace it." Alexei unfolded the square and studied the bullet points. "This is a foreign bank account."

"How do you know?"

"It has a country code at the beginning. Bank accounts in the US do not use this, and I recognize this one. See here, it starts with 'CY'. This is the country code for Cyprus." Alexei folded the paper in half and stuffed it into the side pocket of his mackintosh next to his cigarettes and lighter.

"Why Cyprus?"

"They want to store the money somewhere that there won't be any questions."

"What should I do if I see Pallows again?"

"Shoot her," Alexei said. He stooped down for his coffee on the bench and sipped from the paper cup. It must have been cooling quickly. He looked at it with raised eyebrows and took a longer drink.

"Seriously."

"Only as a last option." Alexei surveyed the path as a walker appeared with a small dog in a vest two hundred yards down.

"I'm not going to shoot anyone," Michael said. His voice took on a lower tone. "I'm just trying to think of what I could tell her to buy time."

"Pretend you are still in play, still a fish on the line." Alexei put his hands together and pretended he was reeling in a fish. "That could keep her satisfied."

"Pallows already has doubts about me from when we met. I told her to come back with a search warrant."

"Damned lawyers. Well done, I'd say. Of course, she won't be able to do that unless she forges something."

"It needs a judge's signature. She could falsify it, but I should be able to distinguish it from the real thing."

"She may also change tack," Alexei said. "They likely aren't aware of the Leamas, but they know of our recruitment efforts and are rushing to cut us off."

"She said you're running guns and ammo, too. Are you?"

Alexei switched into speaking Russian as the walker approached. "No. There's more guns and ammo than they need in Ukraine. The issue is men. You can see she is grasping at things to influence you."

"I didn't understand all of that," Michael said in Russian. They strolled in the opposite direction of the walker.

"You need to keep practicing," Alexei said.

"I don't count on speaking it much more after this."

"Count on it or don't count on it—always be prepared. Do you speak Swedish?"

"My mom made me. It's a hell of a lot easier than Russian. Do you?"

"No, business is done in English."

"Then why would I need to know Russian?" Michael glanced at his companion.

"Because Russian business is done in Russian."

"What do you mean by 'Russian business'?"

"I suppose I mean things that are *po blátu*: using connections and going around standard procedure."

"Do you carry a gun or are you all just trying to make me an assassin now?" Michael asked.

Alexei's laugh rang out into the January sky. "Assassin... Michael, you are our agent of legitimacy. You use the gun we gave you only as a last resort, please."

"So, do you carry or not?"

"I have protection. Don't worry about it." Alexei smiled, waved a hand, and glanced away from Michael for a moment. The cell phone buzzed in his pocket.

"*Allo*," Alexei said. He stopped walking and held the phone tight to his ear. "What?... You're sure? He's with me."

"What's happening?" Michael asked.

Alexei placed the phone back into his pocket and sauntered forward. "Nikolai's car was broken into. His flash drive was stolen."

"What was on it?"

"The passenger list and ship details. We need to get it back before they get past the encryption."

The three gables of the Glensheen Mansion imposed themselves at the end of the driveway that extended from the black iron gate. The gables angled away, discouraging any direct observation. A wet snow had broken out. Its thick clouds took the light, revealing a somberness behind each window of the four stories. The next tour would not begin for another hour. In the absence of visitors, a still cursedness overtook the grounds. There were footprints ahead of them in the slush which disappeared into pavement and did not reappear in snow beyond.

"Has anything changed, Michael?" Pallows asked.

"I wanted to see how you are progressing in your investigation," Michael said.

"I'm still not sure whose side you're on."

"I'm on my client's side until I'm on the side of law enforcement."

"What's the problem? I am law enforcement. You've already waited far too long."

"You know what I mean," Michael said. His eyes caught movement in the trees. A heap of snow fell from a pine branch.

"No, I don't know what you mean."

"Have you obtained a search warrant or evidence that Alexei is about to commit a crime?"

"We recently discovered a vital piece of evidence. We're working to decrypt it now."

"What's the evidence?"

"It will show exactly what and whom Alexei is moving in and out of the harbor."

"Agent Pallows, Alexei may be open to cooperating to help you with your investigation. This could save everyone time and resources."

"No, we are not looking for his cooperation. We don't trust him or his extremist friends. We are looking for *your* cooperation."

A pang of achiness passed through Michael as he registered Pallows' mention of 'extremist.' "Extremist in what way?"

"They are terrorists, Michael." Pallows looked at him with condescension.

The emotion left Michael's face. "Again, if this is a criminal matter, you must consider me his defense counsel."

"What do we need to do in order to convince you a significant crime is about to occur?" Pallows asked.

They arrived at the stone steps of the mansion. Michael gazed up at the engraved, wooden door as if he could command it to open. The subdued glow of the gothic wall lanterns was distorted through clouded glass. "I'm going to need to see the encrypted material."

A brass handle on the inside of the wooden door clapped and a line of visitors proceeded out, passing Michael and Pallows shoulder to shoulder. Michael turned to Pallows and handed her a ripped piece of notebook paper with an address. "Meet me here at seven tonight. Bring what you have." He backed into a narrow gap between two large groups and proceeded away from the staircase.

22

"When did you get here?" Michael asked.

"My flight arrived at six this morning," Mattias said.

The window blinds in the apartment were lowered. Mattias sat in a button tufted armchair under a reading lamp. Sue looked on from the couch across the room. She held a hot cup of tea in her lap, and Michael noticed the kettle on the kitchen table next to two empty cups.

"It's been so nice to meet Sue. I wish I would have been able to make it to the wedding," Mattias said.

"Let's leave her out of this, Mattias," Michael said.

"Of course. We've been waiting for you to talk about a plan."

"A plan for what?" Michael asked. He moved to the table and fixed a cup of tea for himself. The kettle must have just come off the stove. It was light enough to swing, and he wondered if Sue had the same notion.

"For the next couple of days. I think she should leave town for a while. Do you have any family you could visit, Ms. Lund?"

"I'm not going anywhere," Sue said.

"Mattias is right, Sue. You could visit your parents; call in sick to work."

"Why? What's going on?" Sue asked.

"The Leamas will be leaving soon. I think it's best if you are gone between now and then."

"We want to limit any moves that this tiresome pair might make before then," Mattias said.

"You mean the woman who says she is an ATF agent?"

"And her accomplice," Mattias said.

"The man in the Honda?"

"Precisely."

"What do you think they are capable of?" Sue asked.

"We're not sure, but it's about minimizing risk," Mattias said. He crossed one leg over the other and peeled one of the window blinds down to look out. In doing so, his patterned dress socks were exposed. Michael remembered that he never wore plain-colored socks.

"Oh come now, there's a nice sight," Mattias said. "Look at that, will you, Michael."

Michael went to the window and raised the blinds. A red fox tiptoed through the snow, leaving a trail of wily tracks. The light from outside was too weak to brighten the room.

"This town really is how I imagined it. That is, it's something of its own little world. What did Le Carre say about that small town in Germany? A town where the dreams have quite replaced reality?"

"Thanks to you, uncle," Michael said.

Mattias chuckled and tapped his knee. "Well, Michael, the dream is yours, truly. You didn't know my involvement until you accepted this on the merits. Do you understand, now, your calling to the family business?"

"Michael isn't a spy," Sue said. Her hands still cradled the teacup in her lap, but her voice was raised and steady.

Mattias accepted the comment with a tilt of his head. It reminded Michael of his similar tendency.

"Michael is a von Andersson," Mattias said. "This is not only his nature, but his duty."

"Duty to whom?" Sue asked. "To you, Mattias? He doesn't owe you anything, and he doesn't owe your country anything."

"To the righteous, my dear. Wars are fought, governments change, dictators rise and fall. We unflinchingly answer the call to stand up and muster whatever forces we can in the face of evil." He said 'evil' as if it was a supernatural, ever-present force. "On another level, I'm sorry to say that you are incorrect that Michael does not owe our family and our country anything. Michael's duty above all else must be to the family and, ultimately, Sweden. Moving to America only ever gives people another dimension. There is no changing your blood ties and all that comes with it. You live with that connection forever and pass it down through generations. I'm ready for a cup of tea now, please."

"Isn't that what our governments are for?" Sue asked. She remained still.

"Certainly, and in this case, both of our governments are behind the spirit of our cause."

Michael poured a second cup of tea. "It's about more than me, Sue. I have an obligation, and I'm not going to shy away from it."

Sue turned to Mattias and asked, "What will your cause require Michael to do when I leave town?"

"We need to get a flash drive back from Pallows. It identifies the American recruits and ship details," Michael said. "And I need to give the American recruits some assurances that this will all work out."

"I hope you aren't reversing the order of those things," Sue said.

"Us, too," Mattias said. "We plan to get the drive from Pallows tonight."

"Why do you need Michael to get the information back?" Sue asked.

"Because I'm the only one that she vaguely trusts enough to meet." Michael placed the cup of tea on the coffee table in front of Mattias.

"Thank you, Michael. It will be staged as a snatch and grab

theft. Nikolai will go in and take her bag with the hope that she will be carrying the drive inside of it."

"What if it's not in there?" Michael asked.

"Then we re-think the plan, but the ship must sail even if we cannot repossess the drive. There's a chance that they won't ever be able to get by the encryption."

"If they decrypt it, the recruits will be obvious targets when they reach the Black Sea."

"Possibly. It's a high-risk mission, Michael. There was never any doubt on that."

"I want to help," Sue said.

"The best thing you can do for us is to take yourself out of the picture," Mattias said.

"He's right, Sue. Can you go to your parents'?"

"No. I'm going with you to the meeting with Pallows."

"It can't work like that, although your courage is admirable," Mattias said. "I'll tell you what, I will personally keep you updated on the whole matter if you keep a safe distance away."

"How can I trust you?" Sue asked.

"Do you trust that we are on the right side of all of this?" Mattias asked.

"Yes, but the authorities should be involved. This is dangerous."

Mattias uncrossed his leg and reached for his tea. He sipped and pondered, appearing to give Sue's concern due consideration. "That is, of course, a rational proposal, and I do not blame you for bringing it up. However, we are far beyond anything the US authorities could do to help us. It would jeopardize the whole operation and create trouble on an international scale. This is about protecting all of us against a common enemy that is already in an active pursuit to divide us." Mattias sipped his tea again. "If you trust us, we must get you out of here and prepare for the next few hours. They will be pivotal."

23

"It's 18:45," Mattias said. "You have a few minutes still." He glanced at Michael over his newspaper, revealing only his grey, Scandinavian eyes. The elderly barber lathered a man's face with careful brushes, then leaned in with an open razor. Focused. It smelled of menthol proraso shaving cream. Chicago's "25 or 6 to 4" resounded from the stereo at a closed booth at the back of the shop.

"I should go out and wait for her," Michael said.

"If you wish. It's freezing outside," Mattias said. He was engrossed in a local article about elk relocation.

"How's everything else?" Michael asked.

"Oh, it will be fine, the Leamas will make it out on time," Mattias said.

The barber took a step back from the man in his chair and shared a laugh with him through the mirror.

"Nikolai should be in place," Mattias said. "Remember your signals."

"I'm going," Michael said. He stood up from his chair, took a newspaper from the table, and checked that his Carhartt was tucked over the grip of the Smith & Wesson in the waist of his jeans. He was reaching for the door when the barber asked, "Hey, you just come here to steal my paper, son?"

"I was just giving my uncle a ride," Michael said. "I promise I'll bring the paper back."

The barber chuckled and said, "Good, 'cause you know a man like me is good with a blade, I suppose?" The barber held up the razor and winked through his thick, black-framed glasses.

The wind slapped the door shut behind Michael. He hoped it didn't take the barber from his focus. Ahead of him in the brick-laden street, a manhole's steam spilled between passing cars. The smell of shaving cream was replaced by exhaust fumes. He glanced through the window of the barber shop to see Mattias still reading about elk. To warm himself, he strolled along the sidewalk that was also laid with brick. He wore his Red Wings. To keep his toes alive, he exercised them as he walked.

A city bus staggered through traffic to a nearby stop. It slumped over a snowbank and allowed passengers to step directly onto the sidewalk. Pallows was the last passenger to step off. She was alone and carried a nylon satchel over her shoulder. The bus's gears grated against each other as a trail of deep grooves was left in tainted snow.

"Let's take a lap around the block," Michael said.

Pallows held the satchel tight against her hip. "We're still working to decrypt the material we recovered, but I have something else for you."

"A judge's order?"

"No, that would take too long."

"Then what?"

Pallows unzipped the satchel and handed Michael a photo.

Michael switched the newspaper he was carrying to under his left arm. "What am I looking at?"

The photo showed three middle-aged men in the waiting area of an airport gate with large tactical duffle bags beside them.

"These men are thought to be presently in Duluth waiting on orders from the Ukrainian military."

"How do you know that?"

"We spotted them in the Dallas airport boarding a flight for MSP. This is happening, Michael. Now is the time you need to decide which side you are on. We are not going to wait any longer. We need you to provide all the details that you can and plug in our accounts before the money is gone."

"Is this all you are able to show me?" They turned the corner down a side street and walked a narrow, shoveled path in the sidewalk in the direction of the lake.

"This is all we have at the moment."

"I'm not sure this is enough for me to act on."

The door of a parking garage opened behind them. Michael could feel Nikolai approaching. He adjusted the newspaper to stick out further from under his left arm. *Stay away*, he thought.

"You aren't going to leave us with a choice," Pallows said.

"Other than to what?" Michael asked.

"To leave you on the outside looking in," Pallows said. She scoffed and unzipped the satchel to place the photo back inside.

Footsteps grew nearer as Pallows slowed to pull out another item. *Stay away*, Michael said to himself again. He felt the pressure of the Smith & Wesson against his waist.

As Pallows withdrew a black external hard drive, a woman in a stocking cap and running gear brushed by them on the left side and continued jogging down the hill. Michael relaxed his grip on the newspaper.

"Last chance," Pallows said. "Take this hard drive and download whatever files you can from Alexei's computer. If you can't swap out the bank account numbers, this is the minimum expectation."

"I'm not sure Alexei even has a computer."

"Someone does. Make it happen."

Michael took the hard drive and stuffed it into his back pocket. "Where can I find you afterwards?"

"Call me, I'll meet you."

"Where is your office?" Michael asked.

"St. Paul."

"Not Duluth?"

"No, that's a satellite office. You won't find me there. I came up from the main field office. Call me again and we'll set a time and place." Pallows broke away and crossed the street at the end of the block. She took her cell phone out on the other side, made a command, and hung up.

Michael continued around the block and back to the barber shop. It was darker now, or maybe it seemed that way to him. He waited for a break in traffic before fully coming to the door.

"Ah, and he's brought your paper back I see, Roger," Mattias said. He was leaned back in the barber chair with a white towel across his chest. His face was caked in shaving cream, as if it were a mask.

"Never a doubt: I still had you. I could've held you for ransom. Isn't that right?" Roger asked.

Michael's stomach lurched at the thought of kidnapping. "Have you heard anything from Sue, Mattias?"

"He must have been on the phone with his other girlfriend outside. I can't keep track of all your girls, Michael, I've got better things to do."

Roger laughed and leaned away with his razor for a moment as he had done with the previous man. It was a courteous reflex.

"She must've called," Michael said. He withdrew the cell phone from his pocket.

"Yes," Mattias began with feigned reluctance. "We talked on the phone. I told her there has been no change of plans and that you will be able to call her shortly. It sounds like she made it to her parents'. She'll expect a call back."

Michael turned away as Sue answered his call.

"You okay?" she asked.

He told her about the encounter with Pallows in coded terms. Roger was within earshot.

"You're at your parents' then?"

"That's what I told Mattias, but I'm sitting at a gas station outside of Cloquet."

"Why? You should be long gone by now."

"I couldn't do it. I couldn't leave with all of this going on."

"Sue." Michael caught himself before indiscretion took over. "Will you be able to do that for us, please?" He glanced at Roger. He was hard at work again. "Is Kristelena still with you?"

"Yes, but I want you to come with me, Michael. Otherwise, I'll stay."

"I can't do that. You know I'm tied up." Michael walked to the table in the waiting room where it would be harder for anyone to overhear and placed the newspaper gently on top of the pile.

"Are you going to leave me here?"

"Where?" Michael asked.

"In Minnesota."

"No, why would I do that?"

"It seems like the kind of thing that could happen. It's all so out of our control," Sue said.

"I won't leave you stranded. I promise."

"Promise me we'll be together after all this mess is over."

"I promise. We're in it together, like always."

"Is there anything I can do?" Sue asked.

"The best thing you can do is keep yourself safe."

"I keep seeing things, as if I'm being followed. I don't trust anyone I see."

"It'll be done soon, just get to your parents'. And don't trust anyone else."

The door of the shop clanked open. Nikolai stepped inside, letting in the evening chill. He beat the snow off his shoes on the doormat and told Michael 'thank you for the signal' in Russian.

"I'm about done for the night, but I could squeeze you in if you're desperate, son," Roger said.

"I'm okay, just here to visit with these two."

"Well, your man here is about finished," Roger said. He rubbed aftershave between his hands and patted Mattias' freshly shaven face.

Mattias handed him a crisp one-hundred dollar note and thanked him. "Sorry, Roger, I'm a popular man."

"Where are you all from?" Roger asked.

"We've come to this land of opportunity from all corners," Mattias said. "As for my nephew and I, we're Swedish. That other one...God knows." Mattias took his checkered overcoat from the coat tree and fixed the middle two buttons.

"I would've guessed your nephew to be an American."

"He was born here, but he'll always be a Swede."

24

The rattling tin roof of the shed sent echoes across the concrete floors. Most of the cars had a beige dust cover. The few foreign cars that were uncovered were manufactured decades earlier and hardly seemed worth importing or fixing. A green, vintage Defender was missing its driver's side door and had a flat tire. An oily rag was left crumpled under the open hood like a flag of surrender. At the workbench along the wall, four computer monitors were mounted among a mass of black cords that could be traced to two power strips. Pallows' external hard drive sat next to a laptop that was propped up on a thick engine repair manual.

"Why can't you find the recovery key on the laptop?" Pallows asked through the speaker phone, which they sat motionless around.

"The flash drive you have is the key," Michael said back into the phone. "You need the flash drive to get into the laptop. You can take the laptop itself or download the files to the external hard drive." Michael's eyes met the Smith & Wesson sitting on the hood of a car next to him. It stood out sharply in contrast to the car's beige dust cover. He averted his eyes as if Pallows would be able to feel the gun's presence.

"How did you get in the shed?" Pallows asked.

"I know where they keep the key."

"Where are they now?"

"I'm not sure. They're not here right now, and there might not be another opportunity. If they come and ask why I'm here, I'm going to have to lie, but it won't take them long to find out I have no reason to be here."

"Send me the address, we're already in the car."

"Who's we?"

"My partner and I."

"Make it quick."

Mattias held up his fingers and mouthed the word 'five' to Michael.

"If you don't get another call from me in five minutes, call it off," Michael said.

The call ended and Nikolai reached for the Smith & Wesson, placing it in the waistband of his CCM sweatpants. "Are you sure you want to be here for this, Michael?"

"She'll leave immediately if I'm not standing here when she walks in," Michael said.

Alexei pulled out a cigarette but decided against smoking it, perhaps because he thought the smell would linger and knowing that Michael didn't smoke. He placed it behind his ear instead. "Michael should stay. We should all be close," he said. "There will be two of them. We'll have the opportunity to take them both out."

"Take them out?" Michael asked.

"We don't need to make this messier than it needs to be," Mattias said. He was leaning against the hood of another covered car, his arms folded in front of him. "That said, we should be prepared for anything."

"Mattias, is there any chance that these people are actual federal agents?" Michael asked.

"If they were, they would have raided this place and probably your office already. The visit wouldn't have been at your invitation. My contacts have also not been able to identify any agent 'Pallows' with the ATF."

"Maybe she's with another agency," Michael said.

"You saw her badge," Alexei said. "She's a pretender and so is her so-called partner. They are Russian agents."

"If we come on strong and blow their cover, they'll have no choice but to walk away. The Russians will probably try to get in another way, but by that time we'll have picked up and moved shop."

"What do you mean?" Michael asked.

"There's no time to get into that now," Mattias said.

"Of course there is. What do you mean pick up and move shop?"

"We can't stay here after this, Michael. It wouldn't be safe."

"What are Sue and I going to do?"

"Don't worry about that now. We have plans. We'll take care of it." Mattias checked his watch. "You have to call Pallows back in ninety seconds. The rest of us should get into position."

Alexei withdrew a Glock from the inside of his coat and pulled back the slide to put a round in the chamber. His boxcar hands concealed the gun. He moved to the shed door with Nikolai trailing behind. Nikolai withdrew the Smith & Wesson from his waistband and checked the magazine.

Mattias placed a hand on Michael's shoulder. "We're right here with you. Keep your calm. Forty seconds and then make the call."

Alexei flipped off the lights so that only a lamp near the workbench remained on. Michael stood at center stage, blood rushing through him. He checked the Longines. Close enough. He lifted the phone like a twenty-five-pound weight.

"We're still good. Where are you?"

"Almost there," Pallows said. "I'll text you when we arrive. Get us at the door."

Mattias disappeared behind a row of vehicles. The text message took an eternity.

"Here," it read.

Michael placed the phone on the workbench but picked it up again after second thought. He put the phone in his pocket and stepped out of the spotlight through the musty air of the shed, which seemed somehow thicker to him now than before. The door was solid. He put his weight into it, opening it to the night with a screech.

Sue was the first person through the door. Whether from shock or a desire to put the others on notice, he uttered her name aloud. His jaw trembled. Sue's face was skewed and sunken. Pallows appeared closely behind her with a gun buried in the back of Sue's coat. She was followed by the salt and pepper haired man, who held Kristelena at gun point. Michael remained still, as if his feet were stuck in concrete.

"What's going on?" Michael asked.

"I told you that you weren't leaving us with a choice," Pallows said. "Where is the computer?"

"Put the guns down," Michael said. "We don't have to do it like this."

"Show us the computer, or I shoot you now," the man behind Kristelena said. He pressed forward into the shed with his hand on Kristelena's shoulder and a gun at her lower back.

"This is how it's going to go," Pallows said. "Give us what we need and everything will be fine."

The wideness of Sue's eyes grew more evident as she stepped closer to the glow of the lamp. She appeared unharmed, but she was shaking. Kristelena bled from her mouth. The blood collected and dripped in strings from her bottom lip. She gazed straight ahead, as if instructing Michael to keep his focus.

"I'm not doing anything until you put the guns down," Michael said.

"We're here now. We could do the rest without you," the man said.

"I thought you were a federal agent, Pallows. What's going on?"

"We've both lied to each other, Michael." Pallows pushed Sue with the barrel of her gun. Sue shuffled forward with her hands outstretched, ghost white and hollow-cheeked. Michael lunged toward her but caught himself before coming within a threatening distance. He stepped back over the line he imagined.

"Come this way," Michael said. He walked backwards with his palms facing the ceiling and fingers spread apart, steady.

The salt and pepper haired man scrutinized the dark corners of the shed and Michael's open hands. "Tie these two over there," he called to Pallows. He indicated a steel beam with his hooded eyes and a nod.

Before he could turn his head back to Kristelena, she threw an elbow into his abdomen and knocked Pallows to the ground with her shoulder. Michael leapt forward and wrapped his arms around Sue, rushing her behind one of the covered cars as Alexei and Nikolai appeared from the shadows with their guns drawn. A shot was fired, and Michael buckled over the hood of the car, holding himself up with one hand for a moment until rolling onto the ground.

Hearing the footsteps behind him, the salt and pepper haired man turned to Alexei and Nikolai with his gun raised. Alexei fired two rounds into his chest. Pallows, wrestling with Kristelena on the concrete floor, broke free. Desperately, she clawed for the weapon that landed several feet from where she fell.

"Drop the gun," Nikolai said, standing above Pallows as she lay with her cheek against the cold concrete and her bony fingers now outstretched, tense.

"Michael?" Mattias asked, appearing behind Nikolai and Alexei. His hasty steps were underlined by the heels of his leather boots.

"He needs a doctor," Sue said. She stood him up and draped one of his arms over her shoulders, examining him from all angles.

"It's only my shoulder," Michael said. The blood dripped from the wound in a stream down his middle and ring fingers. It was more red than he imagined it would be. The pain set in. His stomach ascended and he stumbled. He braced himself on Sue, whitening.

Sue's hands and cheeks were daubed in blood, and her eyes were piercing. The color had returned to her face. It appeared feverish now. She drew calculated breaths in through her thin nose. "Mattias," she said. She turned her eyes on him, but he must have already understood.

"We must get Michael medical attention," Mattias said. His voice cracked unnaturally and he swallowed hard. "Pallows," he shouted now. "Give us the flash drive. Empty your pockets."

Pallows placed the flash drive beside Nikolai's feet. He picked it up with his gun still pointed at her, inspected it, and threw it to Kristelena. She shoved it into the laptop and punched in the key.

"Where is your wallet?" Mattias asked.

"What are you going to do with me now? I gave you the flash drive."

"It's all here," Kristelena said.

"Where is your wallet?" Mattias asked again.

"It's in the car. Glove box."

Alexei had already searched the dead man's pockets. "Gennady Yagin. Russian Federation passport. Entered the US one year ago. Four credit cards. No badge."

"Where's your badge, Pallows?" Alexei asked.

"What badge?"

"Your counterfeit ATF badge," Alexei said. "The one you showed Michael the other day."

"You know who I work for, and you know they're more dangerous than the ATF." Pallows strained herself to raise her head from the concrete as she spoke. "I'm not a zealot, and I'm not Russian. Let me go."

Alexei knelt close to her face. "Who do you report to?"

"You killed him."

Gennady lay flat on his back, one leg pinned behind the knee of the other. The stiff rubber treads on the bottom of his boots looked new. The snow still melted from them and puddled at his feet.

"Get up slowly, Pallows. We need to leave."

Alexei led them through the door and surveyed the surrounding area. It was a clouded, black night. They could see nothing except the outline of three vehicles.

Nikolai trailed Pallows with the Smith & Wesson. The mixture of snow, ice, and gravel outside of the shed made for uneven ground. As they moved toward the vehicles, Pallows tumbled onto her side, clasped a handful of gravel, and threw it into Nikolai's eyes. She broke away towards the woods to the west.

Kristelena pursued and caught up within ten yards. "Get off of me," Pallows said, as she struggled against her.

"Do we end this now?" Kristelena asked.

"Pallows, it's up to you," Mattias said. "Give us a reason to spare you. Otherwise, we're moving on from this and you can join Gennady inside."

Kristelena removed herself. "She's no use to us, only a threat."

"What's your price?" Pallows asked.

"Tell us what you know. We'll decide if it's good enough," Mattias said.

"You'll shoot me either way." She wiped Kristelena's blood from her face and dusted off her hands.

"I suppose you'll just have to trust us. You don't have any other options it appears."

"They own me. Once they have you, there is no way out. Even if you let me go, I can't guarantee they won't send me back after you. That is, if they still want me operational."

"Give us information. Anything," Mattias said.

"You know we've been tracking the recruitment. We couldn't get into the flash drive. I can tell you that."

"Did you send a copy of the flash drive to anyone?" Mattias asked.

"No, there was no point. It was encrypted."

"We can't believe a word she says," Kristelena said.

"What else can you tell us?" Mattias asked. "I promise you, if you help us, we will let you go."

Pallows put her face into her hands and drew in a deep breath. "They will probably kill me if they find out I told you."

"Die now or maybe die later," Kristelena said. "It's an easy decision."

"Look, I don't know a name, but there is a recruit with you." She trembled and put her hands between her thighs. "Gennady met with him. I wasn't there."

"What about this recruit?" Mattias asked.

"An American?" Alexei added.

"Yes, an American. Ex-military like the others. He has already been to Ukraine, but not as a volunteer soldier. He travelled there and worked odd jobs. My understanding is that he himself engaged the Russian military while he was there. The GRU used him for calling in positions of Ukrainian troops. They've made promises that he can set up a good life in Russia after his service."

"Idiot," Kristelena said.

"He'd be dangerous to you," Pallows said. "I know he's been recruited as part of your effort. He'll be reporting to the GRU on anything his unit does."

"How?" Alexei asked.

"They have contacts everywhere. It wouldn't be over digital comms."

"So they expect him to be arriving in the Black Sea?"

"Yes."

"Do they know what ship?"

"No. He said he wouldn't know the name of the ship until they board. They wouldn't be afraid to sink it either, you know. As soon as it gets to the Black Sea, it's anyone's guess what will happen."

"We need to go to the hospital," Sue said.

"Get Michael in the back of the Volvo," Nikolai said.

Alexei pointed his gun at Pallows. "Are we satisfied, Mattias?"

"What is the GRU expecting to hear from you next?"

"That we broke into the flash drive and accessed the files."

Alexei and Mattias shared a look. Alexei lowered his gun. "Nikolai, take Michael to Gregory. We'll meet you at his office."

25

Michael's vision was blurred from the pain. He lay face down on the reclined dentist chair, now an operating table, hoping for the medication that Gregory shot in his ass to take hold if it had not already. It was as if burning embers lined his back, someone stoking them with a hot iron poker from above. Whether it was real or a figment of his unhinged mind, classical music played in the background. It had no lyrics, only the sweet, oaky sound of a cello, probably Bach. The floor was linoleum and clean. The grey marble tiles were like the surface of a turbulent water. He rose and fell with its waves, clutching onto his raft. But there was another hand on his. Another castaway? The unmistakable daisy scent of Sue's skin and sandy hair was close and displaced the smells of blood, gauze, and other odors of surgery. Her eyes, radiating down like the fresh sunlight of spring, suggested anything but aimlessness: they were foretelling.

"You're almost there, Michael," Sue said. "You're going to be okay."

"What's he doing?" Michael asked. His voice was arid and crackled like an old radio.

"He's just sewing you up now. You're lucky. We're lucky." Sue held a cup of ice water to his lips. He took it in through the paper straw, renewing himself.

Gregory, complete with the surgery, guided Michael upright and wound a bandage around his upper body, above and below his arm. He had a collectedness in all his movements. This, combined with the wild hair of his beard, gave him the appearance of an Eastern Orthodox monk.

"Thank you, Gregory," Alexei said. He stood against a counter that had a grand display of chunky electronic toothbrushes which appeared to be dated by decades. Perhaps there was a commercial reason for the showcase, or perhaps it was a dentist's decoration and was better than having nothing at all.

"Of course. How are you feeling, Michael?" Gregory asked. He sat on the edge of his dentist's stool, hands on his knees and elbows cocked. His eyes were sagged and sensitive.

"Fine, thanks for all your work," Michael said.

Gregory placed a hand on Michael's healthy shoulder, and for a moment Michael thought he was praying.

"Gregory was a medic in Afghanistan; you're not his first gunshot wound," Alexei said. The mention of this had no impact on Gregory. It was a closed matter. The thought of it only a leaf flowing by him on a stream. "Michael, will you be ready to talk to the recruits?"

"You're still going to send them?" Michael asked.

"We can't afford to delay the departure. We have a plan when you're ready," Alexei said. He disappeared into the waiting room.

Mattias and the others loitering in the room when Michael stepped through, repaired and bandaged.

"We heard it was only a flesh wound," Mattias said, coming to his feet. "Thank goodness."

"What's the plan with the ship? Why are you still sending them? They could be sitting ducks once they get to the Black Sea, even if they make it out of Superior on time," Michael said.

"Don't you worry about that, Michael," Mattias said.

"I told him we have a plan," Alexei said.

"What is the plan? Get me to convince them this is safe and then send them to die?"

"Not quite. Actually, Michael, we are going to use the mole to our advantage. You can't hint that we know about him; otherwise, it will throw the whole thing sideways."

"In what way are you going to use him to your advantage?" Michael asked.

"Well," Mattias said. He sat back down in his chair and checked the Lange I watch as if it begged to be consulted. "We aren't for certain who it is, but that doesn't matter. All that matters is we know that there is a mole and that the GRU is expecting the contents of the flash drive. We will give all the recruits the same inaccurate information, which will hopefully be passed to the GRU."

"In addition, Kristelena has fabricated material on a flash drive," Alexei said.

"That's right," Mattias said. "This fabricated information will corroborate and supplement the information we give to the recruits. The materials will be reinforcing."

"What's the false information?" Michael asked. His voice had recovered, and he was able to process matters faster, but his shoulder ached in heavy waves.

"Ports, ships, targets," Mattias said. "The GRU will be led to believe that the Leamas is on one trail of attack, when really it will be on another."

"That would seem to leave open the possibility that the Russians would board or sink the Leamas at any time," Michael said.

"Yes." Mattias wrinkled his brow as if he had something to add, but he declined to go further.

"They wouldn't do that in the Mediterranean," Alexei began. "The danger is in the Black Sea, including mines, which are indiscriminate. The risk is high simply by virtue of sailing in that area, even for civilian ships."

"It's dangerous either way you slice it," Mattias said. He motioned across his body with his index and middle fingers together. It could have been the gesture of a professor during a lecture. "However, it will help if we can draw the GRU's attention away from the ball so to speak."

"We've done what we can to minimize the risk. The command at Blue Scepter is aware of the situation and wishes to proceed. It will be an operational matter from here," Alexei said.

"What were we doing before?" Michael asked.

"I believe they call it counterespionage," Mattias said. He tilted his head towards Michael and smiled, revealing dimples just above his jawline.

"And where does Pallows fit in now?" Michael asked.

"We've let her go in exchange for her help with the deception. She will pretend to have gotten through the encryption and into the contents of the flash drive. It would be suicidal to cross us and tell the Russians about the deal we made. They wouldn't trust her, especially because she was being blackmailed to assist them."

"Was she ATF?" Michael asked.

"She is, but Pallows isn't her real name, and she has been on administrative leave from the agency." The Lange I beckoned Mattias again. "It's time. They'll be waiting for you at the harbor."

26

The profile of Lake Superior waves was visible from the ship deck's weather-beaten railings. A gale wind beyond the canal promised a struggle to any travelers. The signal of the breakwater lighthouse struck peaks of jagged ice as it bobbed up and down, the contours of a ruinous water illuminated by a tint of green. The Soo Locks in Sault Ste. Marie had not closed yet. There were fifteen men in all, dressed not as merchant sailors but already as mercenaries. They all wore a variation of the same attire: a collection of combat boots, drab outerwear, and cold weather gear. Some were clean shaven, some had grizzled beards, and several were somewhere in between. Alexei smoked a cigarette as he leaned against the railing, looking out over the recruits. The air smelled of old iron and stale tobacco.

Michael returned to Mattias' comments as they pulled into an alleyway near the harbor. "They don't need to be overwhelmed by foreigners. You and Alexei go. They need to see a friendly American face. It's good for morale."

"What do I tell them, Mattias?"

"Tell them you worked the transaction involving their funds and it will be ready for them upon arrival. Tell them of the legality of it, if they care, and that they are merely hitching a ride to the

Black Sea on the Leamas, officially joining Blue Scepter upon arrival. Tell them anything, anything except that there is a traitor among them."

Michael stood with his hands interlocked in front of him. His wound burned against the contrast of the cold harbor air. He wished he was smoking next to Alexei, at least then he would be doing something other than standing idle and masking his pain through gritted teeth. Perhaps he looked more trustworthy if he appeared independent, he thought.

"That's everyone," Alexei said. "Why don't you start by telling them about our roles. We can answer questions as needed." He took a slow drag from his cigarette.

By their faces, they could have been a group of passengers whose flight was delayed by several hours. It seemed nothing could be said that would give them value; they only wanted to get to their destination. Anything short of that was an inconvenience. He forged ahead.

"I'm not your lawyer...but I'm an American lawyer who has been working with Alexei through his plans, trying to keep things above board so to speak."

No one laughed. They either didn't think he was joking, or they didn't think it was funny. Michael wrung his hands and shoved them in the pockets of his Carhartt.

"If you haven't met Alexei," he started again, "he is a Ukrainian businessman who has been trying to find a way to contribute in a meaningful way to his country's fight against Russia. In this case, he has arranged for the donation of funds to a non-governmental organization called Free East, which is located abroad and which supports Ukraine's war effort. Free East makes contributions to the Blue Scepter brigade. Any questions so far?"

None of the men raised their hands. "Thank God," Michael whispered to himself. Alexei glanced over at Michael with a confused expression but declined to interject.

"Stop me at any point if there are any questions. I'll be glad to clarify. If you have any doubts about this plan from a legal perspective, though, you should get your own lawyer to advise you. If you have any doubts about your safety in travelling to a war zone and fighting for a foreign nation, you are correct that it is extremely high risk. It is not too late to leave." Michael winced. His wound oozed and his shirt dampened. The recruits, as if smelling blood, grew more attentive.

"Relatedly," he continued, "due to restrictions under applicable federal law, it's important that we all understand you have been recruited by Blue Scepter itself through online channels, located abroad, and that you will formally enlist and receive payment once you reach..." Michael caught himself before offering a more specific destination. "Once you reach Ukraine."

Perhaps the bleeding stopped, or his body was going numb from the second dose of pain medication. "As I said, I'm Alexei's lawyer and so I have assisted Alexei in his business dealings, leading to a donation to Free East. For your purposes, know that Blue Scepter has a reputation as one of Ukraine's most prominent, well-funded brigades. My understanding is Free East supports them frequently. Practically, Alexei's donation to Free East will give your wages a boost. What else...are there any questions?"

A man with a brown beard and dark eyelashes grumbled as he stroked his chin. "Will Blue Scepter or the Ukrainian government tell the US government that we are joining the foreign legion?"

Alexei smashed his cigarette into a mooring chock and stepped from the ship's railing, his mackintosh rippling in the breeze. "No, they will not tell the US government that you have volunteered. They keep these things confidential."

"But, of course," Michael said, "if you document your experience on social media, it will be public knowledge, so don't post."

"Do not post about your experience," Alexei said. "Most important aspect about this will be to prevent the Russians from knowing your activity and potentially tracing your unit. Also, if they find your posts, you expose yourself and your whole network to Russian trolls."

"How do we know we are going to get paid a bonus? Will that be in our contract with Blue Scepter?" A man in a fleece beanie asked.

"Yes," Michael said. "Make sure the contract you sign with Blue Scepter shows all the money you are expecting."

"How do we know they will follow the contract?"

"You don't," Michael said.

"Unless there is a surrender by Ukraine, you will get paid," Alexei said. "This brigade has strong financial support from the west. If money dries up, more will come, do not worry about it, my friend."

"Is there backing from the US?"

"No," Alexei said.

"Then from who?"

"From other countries in the west, in Europe."

"Which ones?"

"It is not your concern. It's best if we do not provide this information. For your purposes, know that there is strong support for Blue Scepter."

"What is the plan when we arrive to the Black Sea?"

"You will call at port, which is still undecided. From there, the specifics of your missions are operational matters that command at Blue Scepter will have to communicate."

"Understood, thank you." The man removed his beanie and ran his fingers through his young black hair. "Is it still the case that we are to target ships sailing in the Russian shadow fleet?"

"That is what has been communicated to me," Alexei said. "You will be part of a sabotage unit."

"Are we going to receive material on the targets so that we can study the ships' infrastructure?"

"Again, this will have to be communicated to you by command upon arrival and formal enlistment." Alexei tucked his hands into the front pockets of his mackintosh and looked down to his mist-covered, leather shoes. "However," he began again and stared over the lake, "I understand the initial run will be on oil tankers on Turkey's northern coast." Alexei pulled a small, hard-cover note-book from his coat pocket. "AKD Management is a Turkish shipping company that is controlled by the Russian GRU. Their office is located in Istanbul. They have numerous tankers that transport Russian oil in order to get around the sanctions. Our people have identified this as a key target. Blue Scepter will identify the specific ships that will be your subject."

The disarray of the apartment was evident even in the charcoal grey light of the early morning. A framed wedding portrait of Michael and Sue lay shattered beyond the door, its splintered glass web reflecting the hallway bulb. Bookshelves were peeled clean from the meaty law books on the bottom row to the eclectic paperback collection on the top. Pages were torn from what appeared to be a hasty, yet thorough, search. Two of the kitchen chairs were knocked over. The cupboards were agape.

"Wait here," Michael said. He knelt to pick up the wedding portrait.

"What happened?" Sue asked. Her chest rose and fell with her breath.

"Someone has been here. Probably looking for anything to do with Alexei."

Michael stepped into the living room from the entry way. The keys still dangled from the lock.

"Don't go in any farther," Sue said from the doorstep. She grabbed him under the arm and pulled him back to her hip. "We shouldn't be here, Michael. Let's leave and call the police."

"We should call Mattias," Michael said. He set the black and white wedding portrait on the shelf face-up, catching a glimpse of Sue's sanguine smile.

"He's the one who got us into this mess," Sue said through strained lips.

"I got us into this, and I'm sorry for that, Sue. Stay here, I need to see how bad this is."

Michael switched the light on and stretched over the broken glass. He was weightless as he re-traced a set of wet shoe prints punched into the carpet. A lamp in the office beamed against the cream-colored wall as if arranged for a shadow play. The desk was ravaged. Documents and pages ripped from notebooks were scattered across the floor and into the four corners of the room. Closer to the desk now, his shadow appeared on the wall behind him, doubling his figure. He took a screwdriver from the drawer and applied it to the aluminum air-vent grid underneath the desk. Alexei's file was still fastened to the bottom of the vent with a strip of duct tape. Michael jolted it free and tucked it under his injured arm. He replaced the grid and screws, turning them halfway.

"Did they go through everything?" Sue asked, leaning in through the doorway.

"They went through my desk and shuffled through all the documents I had, but they didn't see everything."

"What's under your arm?"

"Alexei's file. I started hiding it after Sweden."

"What are we going to do, Michael?"

"You may not like it," Michael began. He braced himself on the shelving next to the door, at all costs averting his gaze from the shattered wedding portrait. "I think you should leave me and take yourself out of this."

Sue's eyes grew large. "Never say that. I know things are bad. Based on everything we've gone through, what makes you think I would leave you now?"

"I'm serious, Sue. You shouldn't be involved with this. It's my fault. You have the chance to get away, and that would be the smart thing to do."

"I'm not leaving you." She put her hands at her waist and curled her lips. "But you have to make a choice, Michael. You have to end this or end us."

"I don't know where things are going to go from here, but the best option is to continue on with Mattias. Calling the authorities might put a stop to everything, but the implications would be too drastic."

"You would rather walk away from this relationship than this situation?" It was an accusation, not a question.

"It's not that simple." Michael closed his eyes. They were heavy and stung at the corners. He could have slept upright if he had the time. When he opened his eyes a moment later, Sue's unsatisfied gaze was still fixed on him.

"Sue, I don't know how I let things get this far. All I wanted to do was help Alexei raise some money to bring help to Ukraine. It seemed like such a small part to play, a small risk to take."

"Michael, I love you for your heart." Sue brought his hands tight into her chest. "All that matters right now is us. Right here."

Michael gripped her hands. She gripped them back. "We are out of options, Sue. We should leave, and Mattias can help us with that."

"Do you mean leave the country?"

"Yes."

"Forever?"

"For the time being. My life may never be the same, but at least we can be together. Is that enough for you?"

"What do you mean your life may never be the same? What will it mean to continue on with Mattias?"

"He can protect us, but I can't live a normal life anymore, or at least not now."

"What will he want in return?"

"I'm not sure. But we've already helped his cause, and he is family. He will help us. Will you come with me?"

Sue brushed the hair back gently from her face and curled it behind her ear. Michael kissed her on the top of her head, taking in her daisy scent for what he hoped wouldn't be the last time. "Please come with me," he said.

Sue kissed his hands and looked up with resoluteness. "Call Mattias."

Michael drew his phone from his pocket. "Are you sure?"

She nodded. "Speaker phone, please, I want to hear him."

Mattias answered on the third ring. The line crackled.

"What is it?" Mattias said.

"Someone was here. They were at our apartment, searching through things. It's a mess."

"Time to get you out."

"Where?"

"Anywhere but here for now. And Sue?"

Michael looked to her. She nodded again. "Yes, she's coming."

"I'm here for both you and Sue. You have a side in this. You have support."

"Which side is that?" Michael asked.

"The good side, of course."

"It wasn't you, was it?" Michael asked.

"For what? The apartment search?"

"Yes, you didn't even ask if they found anything."

"You and Sue are my main concern. I have no reason to search your apartment, do I?"

"What if I was actually working with the authorities?" Michael asked.

"Then you better let me know so I can get on the next plane," Mattias said, growing impatient. "We have only told you so much information to protect you in situations like this, Michael, and to protect the operation. What do you think they found? Anything?"

Michael let his accusation go. "They didn't get anything. I taped Alexei's file down in the air vent."

"Good lad, just like I taught you."

"What's next, Mattias?"

"We wait to see smoke."

"What do you mean?"

"Talk soon."

27

Their luggage crowded the bar of the breakfast diner. The waitress scowled at them as she slid a plate of pancakes onto the counter and slapped down a sticky syrup dispenser out of reach. Spatulas clanked against the griddle in the background, mixing with the sound of sports radio. It smelled of hashbrowns and strong coffee. Michael sat on the edge of the stool, his shoulder throbbing.

"Take this," Sue said, holding her hand out with two white pills. "Gregory sent us away with some."

"You've been holding out on me?" Michael asked, taking the pills and chasing them with the soapy diner water.

"I'm a nurse. I'm taking care of you," Sue said. She was glowing somehow despite the lack of sleep.

"The car will be here in ten minutes to take us to the airport," Mattias said. "Eat quickly."

"Where are we going?" Michael asked.

"You'll stay at the country house outside of Stockholm for now. Just don't touch the artwork, it's been in our family for hundreds of years."

"Why would I touch the art?"

"You're wearing a Carhartt with what appear to be old blood

stains, not sure from what ...you seem like the kind of person who touches art in museums. Come to think of it, leave that coat here, too, will you?"

"It's my favorite coat," Michael said. "It's broken in perfectly."

"You should try to blend in when you get to Stockholm, not look so *midwestern*." Mattias waved his hand with a flourish when he said 'midwestern,' probably knowing it would set Michael off.

Michael shot him a look of annoyance, and Mattias put a hand on his shoulder. "I'm kidding, bring whatever you like."

"What about the others?" Michael asked.

"Who? The dentists and Alexei have their own plans, as do you."

Michael paused and asked under the noise of the diner, "What did you mean about watching the smoke?"

"Last night, Alexei advised the recruits that they would be heading to Turkey's northern coast, but actually, they aren't going there. He said it would be AKD Management's ships. This is a diversion. The flash drive that we gave to Pallows says almost the same thing, except no mention of AKD Management. They aren't going to northern Turkey, and they aren't targeting AKD Management. AKD doesn't send ships to the Baltic. We don't care about them. We will watch the reaction and see if any moves are made around AKD, then we will know if the game has been bought."

A busy cook yelled from the kitchen, "Eighty-six on rye."

The waitress, punching figures into the cash register, turned and snapped back, "How are we out of rye?"

"I already told you we were running low," the cook said in frustration. "The next shipment is late."

Michael leaned over to Mattias, his fingers tracing his upper lip. "How will you pick out the traitor among the recruits?"

"We don't want to do that just yet," Mattias said.

"What a damn mess. This whole week," the waitress said, as she scribbled down amounts onto a diner guest check.

"Why not?" Michael asked. "Isn't that dangerous to have someone like him involved?"

"It's not our problem anymore, Michael," Sue said. "We're done with this." Sue sat over her untouched plate of pancakes and eggs.

"You should eat something, Sue," Mattias said. "No one likes airplane food."

"You didn't answer the question, Mattias," Michael said.

"You heard Sue, Michael. She's right. This is out of your hands. It's out of my hands as well. The Leamas has successfully left the harbor without raising any eyebrows, and it will barely make it out of Superior before the season closes. We both did our jobs; now it's time for the others to take things from here. It's not your problem anymore."

"No, what's the plan? I need to know."

"We will keep giving misinformation until that seems to not work anymore. At that point, it will be like the pirates," Mattias said, a twinkle in his eye as he applied a fork and knife carefully to his pancakes.

"What the hell does that mean?" Michael asked.

"You know, some of the crew will deal with it once they narrow down the suspects."

"He'll walk the damn plank or what?"

Mattias took a sip from his black coffee and sighed. "He'll be thrown overboard in the night."

"Is that what you're going to do with us?" Sue asked.

"Heavens no, Sue," Mattias said, chuckling. "We are family. We are in this together." Mattias became serious as he withdrew a crisp one-hundred dollar note from his pocket and put it at the edge of the counter. Standing, he savored a last sip from his coffee. He surveyed the diner, one hand on his hip and the other holding his coffee. He checked the Lange 1 and set the heavy-bottom coffee mug on top of the one-hundred dollar note. "Nikolai is here with the car," he said, and sat down once more. Now he leaned into Michael and Sue. "I know this has been frustrating, but none of us can know the full picture. We can't know the complete truth. It's impossible. We just make the best judgments we can with our own little perception of the world, based on the few we choose to trust. I can tell you this: I can't protect you if you stay here, and if you come with me, you're with us. Time to trust me. Time to accept your role, your duty. The time has been ticking away, Michael. Tick tock." Mattias stood and lifted his leather duffle bag onto his shoulder. "If you're ready, I'll see you outside."

Michael rubbed his thumb over the Longines. He took Sue by the hand. "Still with me?"

"Until the end."

ALSO BY WILLIAM BRENNAN

Michael Lund Series

Chasing Truth in a Harbor Town

Never miss a new release!

To find out more about William Brennan and his books, visit

severnriverbooks.com/collections/william-brennan

ACKNOWLEDGMENTS

I am grateful to Julia Hastings, Patricia Graves, and the rest of the publishing, editing, and design team at Ten Hut Media for their guidance and expertise. Most of all, I am grateful to my wife, Megan, for her unending support and inspiration.

ABOUT THE AUTHOR

William Brennan is the pen name of William Bigham. He is a lawyer and lives in outstate Minnesota with his wife. William attended the universities of Minnesota–Duluth, Minnesota–Twin Cities, and Uppsala (Sweden).

Similar to many Minnesotans, hockey has served as a link to places and people for him. From junior hockey in the Rockies, to local pickup games in Sweden, William gained an appreciation for how the game channels great stories and celebrates storytelling.

William is an avid traveler and has a particular connection with Sweden, having lived, coached, studied, and gotten engaged in the country.

Learn more about William's books at
severnriverbooks.com/collections/william-brennan

instagram.com/william.brennan.writer

www.ingramcontent.com/pod-product-compliance
Lightning Source LLC
Chambersburg PA
CBHW031235260626
47169CB00007B/2310